CONFESSIONS

of an elf

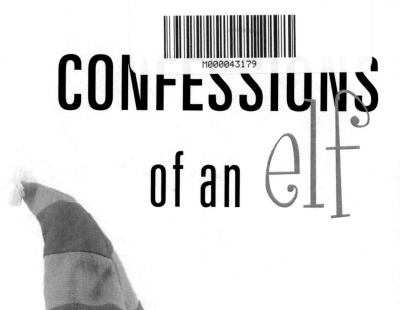

CONFESSIONS
of an elf

Ira David Wood III

TATE PUBLISHING
AND ENTERPRISES, LLC

Published by Tate Publishing & Enterprises, LLC
127 E. Trade Center Terrace | Mustang, Oklahoma 73064 USA
1.888.361.9473 | www.tatepublishing.com

Tate Publishing is committed to excellence in the publishing industry. The company reflects the philosophy established by the founders, based on Psalm 68:11,
"The Lord gave the word and great was the company of those who published it."

Book design copyright © 2011 by Tate Publishing, LLC. All rights reserved.
Cover & Interior design by Leah LeFlore

Published in the United States of America

ISBN: 978-1-61346-767-1
1. Fiction / Fantasy / Contemporary
2. Fiction / General
11.11.02

TABLE OF CONTENTS

For Ashley

INTRODUCTION

Grasp the subject. The words will follow.

—QUINTUS ENNIUS

Before you read another word in this book, you're going to have to accept four things as fact:

1. My name is Marvin.
2. I'm an Elf.
3. I live at the North Pole.
4. I work for Santa Claus.

Now, I don't think anyone should have any difficulty with number one. (Except for those of you who labor under the mistaken impression that all of us elves have cute little names like the Seven Dwarfs.) Numbers two through four, on the other hand, are definitely going to give a few of you some major trouble. If that's your case, you are what we call a nonbeliever.

If you are a nonbeliever, there's no reason at all to feel defensive. This book isn't intended to change your mind. It's not my job to try to make you believe in anything. Either you do or you don't. It's really that simple. So just relax and try to keep up, okay?

If you had no problem at all accepting my first four statements, you're what we call a believer. (Congratulations!) Either way, I'm still going to ask all of you to finish reading this introduction. It's just a matter of establishing some common ground between us.

The truth is that most human beings believe in things because they choose to. They choose not to believe in some things for the very same reason. And it doesn't matter whether something they believe in happens to be scientifically provable or not. Human beings simply believe what they want to believe. What's more, they clearly have a habit of accepting information that confirms that belief while tending to reject information that conflicts with it.

Proof tends to be what most rational human beings use to defend their choice of beliefs. The trouble is everyone seems to have a little bit of proof to support whatever they choose to believe in. It's been something of a human stalemate for a long time now.

The very tough part about all this believing/nonbelieving business is that it all finally boils down to a question of faith. And I'm not referring to what we, at the North Pole, call ORC—obvious religious connotations. In fact—if you don't mind—I'd like to keep the obvious religious connotations as far away from this preliminary discussion as possible.

I certainly understand the complication here because we also happen to be dealing with the subject of Christmas. But that's not what this book is really about—at least not what might be considered mainstream ORC. After all, it's going to be enough of a leap for most of you to simply accept the fact that I'm an elf! So let's just say believe what you want to believe and let it go at that for the time being, okay? Thank you.

A word of caution, now, to you believers: this book isn't exactly going to be a romp through the tulips for you either. It's not going to be as easy as simply being asked to clap your hands if you believe in Tinkerbell. You're going to have to commit to a bit more affirmative action where the world's spiritual apathy is concerned. Just wanted you to know that up front.

And, please, as long as we're putting it all on the line, let me say that this isn't as much a book for children as it is a book for the childlike virtues inside all humans regardless of their age. So if the children in your lives are ready for what this book has to say, by all means share it with them. If not, there's really no need to burden them with your doubts. They'll be able to read this by the time they need to hear what it has to say.

One final word of advice to you believers: the world isn't in the best shape right now. That's one of the main reasons I decided to break the Elfin Code of Silence to write this book.

And believers are just as guilty for the condition of the world as nonbelievers—probably more so. In some situations that statement happens to be cause for celebration. In other cases, it isn't.

I'll be very honest with you; I'm probably going to catch some flak for writing all of this down and getting it into print, but it happens to be my personal opinion that the contemporary world—your world—has really lost touch with Santa Claus, and it just seems to me that we need him more than ever right now. More than that, you need an image of Santa Claus that fits into your present lifestyles. In most cases, everyone still seems to be saddled with the old clichéd images of that "right jolly old elf" Mr. Clement Moore wrote about in 1822. Well, we are ... and we aren't. I mean, do you remember how Santa Claus was dressed in Mr. Moore's poem? "All in fur ... from his head to his foot." Fur! Not red felt or even velvet. Well, who are we talking about there? Santa Claus or Daniel Boone? Fur is fur. And fur is a lot of things. But one thing fur isn't ... is red. Not even fox fur is really red. Not red like the red in Santa's suit ... at least not the Santa suit you've come to know over the years.

Don't get me wrong. "The Night Before Christmas" is truly a wonderful poem ... and Santa can be anything you really want him to be. I mean, after all, he was born out of our need for him and for everything he represents to mankind. It was the German born illustrator, Thomas Nast, who actually gave the world its visual impression of Santa in his beautiful illustrations for *Harper's Weekly*—a magazine that was very popular in the 1860s. Believe it or not, the earliest illustration by Nast depicts Santa Claus visiting a Union Civil War camp. It appeared in the January 3, 1863 edition of *Harper's Weekly* and shows Santa Claus in a sleigh, being pulled by reindeer. In 1931 an artist by the name of Haddon Sundblom created Santa's final makeover for Coca-Cola Enterprises. Sundblom's Santa was dressed in the traditional red suit trimmed with white fur but appeared more cheerful and robust than Nast's original drawings. So it was an illustration for a soft-drink manufacturer's marketing campaign that finally came to define Santa Claus as the world now knows him.

Well, c'mon. Let's be realistic here. There've been just a few changes in fashion since 1822—or 1931 for that matter! But popular perception hasn't allowed this man to truly update his image (or wardrobe) in well over a hundred years! (Even though it's probably just as well that he was never overly fond of bell-bottom trousers.)

What I'm trying to say is: if you need Santa Claus to wear the red suit, he wears the red suit. But I also happen to know that he's just as comfortable in an old, gray sweatshirt, a pair of khaki pants, and his fleece-lined slippers. The point is: it's really all up to you!

Just remember that needing Santa Claus is only part of it—the easiest part, in fact. You also need to define him for yourself. And it's not a good idea to allow others to do that part of it for you. One man's trash can very well be another man's treasure. Take it from an elf who knows.

Your concept of the spirit of Christmas—like your concept of God—is a very personal thing. You also have to guard against being too willing to believe in everything that falls into your lap. That isn't always a mark of wisdom.

For instance, if you accepted, without question, the four statements I made at the very beginning of this introduction, you were wrong!

My name isn't Marvin!

THE WORLD IS FULL OF ELVES

Genuine belief seems to have left us.

—WALT WHITMAN

When humans are born into the world, they are what we call "littles." When they grow up, they become "biggles"—and the time it takes for a little to become a biggle is never exactly the same for every single person. This is because a person's age really has nothing to do with whether or not they have become a biggle or they haven't. Humans will tell you otherwise, of course. This is because humans measure their growth in years.

After a certain number of years pass, littles (whether they want to or not) are simply expected to become biggles and shift over into a world where less than 65 percent of the people in it are happy! And, by the way, American biggles are, on average, only 69 percent happy, but they consider happiness more important to them than money, moral goodness, and even going to heaven.

The interesting thing about this process of growing is that the little never stops existing. Some biggles don't like to believe this, but it's true. The little part of a person is always there; the biggle part eventually develops around it. Humans call this "growing up," but, as you see, it's really a matter of actually growing around. When this happens, it's sometimes very hard to still be able to find the little part of a person. That's why some people think the little part has gone forever. But it never does! It's always there—hidden away—deep inside.

Some biggles forget this. But then, some biggles forget so many things. A good many biggles have even forgotten what it was like to be a little! Can you imagine what Christmas time must be like for them?

Now, for some people, the change from little to biggle happens very quickly. For others, the change is much slower and often takes a bit of effort. For a few—for a very, very special few—the change never really happens at all. Oh, they may have biggle bodies, but the little never got lost inside of them—and they are the most special biggles of all!

Biggles are not generally aware that the world is full of elves. But then, most biggles are not really aware of a lot of things. Many biggles simply "have knowledge" of something. Of course, "having knowledge" is very commendable in its place. There are people who work rather hard at it and take enormous pride in believing they have more knowledge than others. It's just that "having knowledge" doesn't necessarily mean that someone is particularly aware of anything.

I honestly don't think it will come as a shock that a great many biggles seem to be afflicted with "having knowledge" without awareness ... and that makes it especially hard on elves. Because while most biggles have some knowledge of elves, they're still not absolutely sure we exist. On the rare occasion when we actually find a human being willing to admit that elves do exist, they too often qualify their testimonies by adding that we exist only in their imaginations.

Okay, let me ask you a question. Do airplanes exist? Can we assume most of you are aware that they do? More to the point, can you even imagine your world without them?

Well, there was a time—and I remember it quite well—when airplanes did not exist. What's more, the world got along quite nicely without them. There was once a time when, on Christmas Eve, littles pressed their wide-eyed faces against frosty, candle-lit windowpanes to gaze with breathless wonder into starry night skies. Why? Because there was once a time when children knew that only Santa Claus could fly. The star-sprinkled Christmas Eve skies of yesterday belonged to him alone. It's almost impossible, now, to understand just how glorious the thought of a flying sleigh used to be to the littles of the world.

Speaking of airplanes, have you ever wondered why Orville and Wilbur Wright chose the month of December to make their first flight at Kitty Hawk? They discovered what we elves have known for a long time—the winds are better for flight during December! If you don't believe me, ask a reindeer.

Consider, too, that—once upon a time— Orville and Wilbur were littles too. They lived in the world I just described. Have you ever wondered how the thought of manned flight originally occurred to them? It's just possible that the idea was first born on a Christmas Eve long ago while two young brothers stood in breathless wonder, faces pressed against a frosty window pane, gazing up together into a starry night sky.

Don't you see? Before it became a reality, manned flight had to first be imagined. Imagination is the very source of all your creativity!

In fact you only have to glance back at your history books to understand that once human beings begin to imagine impossible things, it's not long before they find some way to make those dreams possible.

The thought of elves being real has existed in people's imaginations certainly as long as the thought of flying … even though people once said that both ideas were impossible. And just look what happened with flying! So to say that elves are real in your imagination is almost as good as saying elves are real … period. You don't need to understand how; just enjoy the fact that we are.

Most biggles don't believe in elves because they've forgotten how much fun it used to be when they could believe. Littles, for instance, can watch a magician perform—and absolutely believe that what they're seeing is magic. Biggles, seeing the same thing, often spend their time trying to figure out the trick.

Sir Herbert Read said that " … in the process of education … we are psychically deformed because we are compelled to accept a social concept of normality which excludes the free expression of aesthetic impulse." In other words, being a biggle can sometimes be a real bummer!

A very wise man once said that the price of wisdom is sorrow. That's because having knowledge can sometimes take away the magic. On the other hand, imagination, inventiveness, and fantasy can often bring our dreams to life with wondrous truth and power. Sadly enough, the worst thing a little will eventually learn in this world is how to begin to doubt. When that happens, it's a sure sign that childhood is soon coming to an end.

Most biggles have a habit of doubting things they don't understand. I just don't think biggles realize how much energy it takes to keep doubting. If they did, we'd certainly have more believers in the world than we do now. I suppose most people think you have to understand something before you're able to enjoy it. And I freely admit to once harboring that same belief myself; but something occurred one day that changed the way I thought about everything.

Let me tell you how it happened.

We elves at the North Pole generally refer to Santa Claus as "the boss." Well, one day the boss came into the workshop with a brand new toy. It was a wonderful thing with wheels and levers and buttons. When you turned it on, it moved!

Absolutely fascinated, I studied that toy for hours, trying to figure out how it worked. I couldn't!

Finally taking it back to the boss, I explained my frustration. He merely smiled and leaned back in his chair.

"Do you like grapes?" he asked me with a twinkle in his eye.

"Yes, I do." I answered.

"Do you understand grapes?" he asked.

I paused to think for a moment. Nobody had ever asked me that question before.

"Well, no," I finally replied, "now that I think about it, I guess I don't really understand grapes at all."

The boss leaned forward in his chair, the way he does when he has something very special to say.

"Still enjoy grapes, though, don't you?" he said with a wink. The boss had a point. I do enjoy grapes a great deal. "So," he smiled, "maybe you should give that toy another try."

I took his advice. Well, that wonderful new toy and I went back into the workshop, and I spent the whole afternoon just playing with it—enjoying what it was without worrying anymore about having to understand how it worked. And do you know what happened? After awhile, it was as if the simple act of enjoying it began to open up all of its hidden mysteries to me. I even began to understand it!

Now, elves are smart, but we don't know everything. So whenever we do learn something new, we tend to celebrate it. And that day was a real celebration for me—I can tell you that!

It's always been amazing to me how many biggles will sit quietly together on Christmas morning, watching littles playing with their new gifts. If you look closely, just behind their smiles, you'll notice something identical in practically every pair of biggle eyes. If it isn't sadness, it's certainly something very, very close to it.

Do you know why? I think, secretly, those biggles would love nothing more than to sit down on the floor and enjoy being a little again—just one more time. Most of them never do, of course, but only because they don't allow themselves to listen to the little who's still alive inside of them. That short, healing distance from the sofa to the floor becomes one of the hardest, most difficult moves in any biggle's life. There are times when the little inside of every biggle would like so very much to come out and play. I think it's such a shame they're not often allowed that privilege and pleasure ... most especially at Christmas time.

Biggles are biggles after all—and as near as I've been able to decipher it, there seems to be some sort of unspoken code that begins to dictate what a biggle can or cannot do. I don't think anybody ever wrote it down anywhere. Biggles just seem to somehow learn about it and spend the better part of their biggle years trying very hard to follow it. Most of them don't even know why. It seems they do it simply because everyone else appears to be doing it. Most people, however, fail to notice that no one else seems to be having a particularly happy time, so everyone just keeps on doing it. An empty cycle is therefore passed from one generation to the next.

The puzzling thing is that every human being is a unique individual. No two of you are ever exactly alike. It's the way you're made! Yet most of you will spend your lives trying as hard as you can to be just like everybody else! Oh, it's one of your best excuses for everything. "Well," you say, "everybody else does it." Or, "Everybody else has one."

So with everybody spending all their time trying to do things they don't honestly want to do, everything has finally become so confusing that humans have even invented special kinds of doctors just to help them figure out why they eventually become so unhappy.

As far as biggles are concerned, elves have a lot of things going against them. We may, on first glance, appear to be nothing more than a bunch of subordinate Clauses, but the simple fact is the world is full of us. Biggles just don't want to admit it! I suppose their reasoning is that nobody else believes in elves. So, once again—they just drift along with the mainstream. This is something they like to call "maturity."

Elves have a few fans, of course. JRR Tolkien, Will Ferrell, and that game called Dungeons and Dragons certainly gave us a boost in the public-relations department. But then again, there's a difference between Tolkien elves and Christmas elves. You won't find a single Christmas elf living in Middle-Earth, and not one of us understands or speaks the Sindarin language. Additionally, an Isuzu Elf is not an elf; it's a truck. Elf Aquitaine is not a drink; it's a French oil company.

Still, in all fairness, I can't put all of the blame for the existing confusion on biggles. Ever since they were littles, they've only seen pictures of us in fairy tale books, where we have pointed little ears, beards, skinny legs, and wrinkled tights—sort of a visual cross between Shakespeare and *Star Trek*. Well, face it; you just don't see too many people walking the streets wearing outfits like that—at least not since the sixties ended—every day. Imagine your reaction if you did!

I'm certainly not implying that we don't ever wear tights and beards—or even those stupid little pointed hats with a bell attached to the tip. We do—sometimes—but not always ... and certainly not when we visit the world of humans! (Remember: it's not our job to prove that we exist.) When we visit the world of humans, we dress exactly the way you dress. In fact, I have to admit to actually enjoying the occasional current fashion statement.

Here's something I'll bet you've never considered: when we visit your world, we don't just wear what you wear—we actually look like you too. We can do that, you know. We learned it from Santa Claus. He does it all the time!

Have you ever dropped something on a busy sidewalk and had someone pick it up and hand it back to you? The chances are very good that the person who did it was an elf—in human form! Most of the "people" who take the time in crowded department stores to help lost littles find their mothers are actually elves. You've probably bumped into Christmas elves hundreds of times without even realizing it!

Want to know why we do it? Why we pay these little visits to your human world? I'll tell you. (And you can call it an experiment in elfin psychology if you want to, but it's the truth.) We do it because we've learned quite a bit about the way human minds work. We even figured most of it out before you ever came up with the idea of "psychologists."

Here's the deal. Since we know that you always seem to do things simply because other people are doing them, we came up with what I think is a very clever strategy. Suppose—just suppose—you saw what you thought were people doing nice things for others. Being human, you'd simply assume that everybody else was doing nice things for other people. And since humans don't like to be different from anybody else, sooner or later you'd join the crowd. That's what we decided, at any rate. And we were right!

I'm not saying that humans only learn to do kind things for each other as a result of elfin influence alone. Not at all. If everybody still has a little living inside of them, that means everyone also harbors some bit of innate kindness as well— especially around Christmas time.

Because Christmas is a time when the little in you always stirs—and most often speaks directly to your heart. What's more, Christmas is one of the few times you tend to pause and honestly listen.

What happens as a result? You begin to feel better inside. For a moment—for one simple, beautiful moment—it doesn't matter whether or not anyone else around you is doing something kind or even says "thank you" because you're doing it. You do it anyway—and that's what counts. No one really has to know. No one has to even notice.

But here's something else. (And it's the main reason you should never doubt the existence of elves in your world.) Christmas time, aside from everything else, is a time when human spirits seem to join together in some glorious, unspoken bond the world over. We don't have to understand how it happens; all we have to do is try to be aware of it—when it does happen—and just enjoy the happening!

It's not as difficult as you may think. Sometimes it's only a matter of slowing down the hectic pace of everyday life. Often it's a matter of simply taking some time away from what you usually spend most of your lives concentrating on. Otherwise, you're only blindly following the unspoken Biggle Code of Behavior that finally only leads to empty promises and a lonely heart.

Our time is finite. Our kisses under the mistletoe aren't unlimited, you know. That number is also finite and set by an old tradition. According to the custom, which began long ago in England, each time a kiss is claimed under a mistletoe bough, the young man is supposed to pick off a berry. When all the berries are gone, there's no more kissing. Over the years we've somehow managed to fool ourselves into thinking that, like kisses under the mistletoe, our time on this earth is also unlimited.

Littles are lots of things. But of all the things a little is or ever can be, a little is love. Pure and simple love. To say we draw closer to the little inside of us at Christmas time is to say we also draw closer to the love inside of us. Whenever we do just one small act of kindness, we set free a bit of that love. We let it go out into a world that so desperately needs it.

Now, I'm going to let you in on a great secret. It's the simple proof that elves do exist—that the world is actually full of them. All you have to do is open your heart wide enough to accept a brand new idea.

It's just this:

If a little is love ... and if all of you still have a little inside of yourselves ... then all of you also have the ability to love unconditionally. You never grow too old to love. You will never go so far away that love's light can't guide you safely back home again.

Whenever you commit a single act of kindness, unseen or unappreciated though it may appear to be, you bring a bit more of that loving light into the world. In that brief moment of your life, wherever you are and for whatever you are doing that's kind, you become an elf! You do! It's probably happened to you already without you even knowing it!

When it happens ... when you add just one act of kindness to the world, it's as though you light a candle in some dark place. In that instant, the true spirit of goodwill toward men becomes stronger and brighter everywhere. The love within that light pushes a little more of the darkness away.

A seven-year-old once said, "Love is what's in the room with you at Christmas if you only stop opening presents and listen."

That's why Christmas is always such a cherished time— because, at least for one single day out of the entire year, we allow ourselves to reclaim the happiness of youth whether we happen to be elves or people. When that happens, we suddenly become wonderfully aware of things again! You can't help it! It's almost as if we are able to see, hear, touch, taste and feel the world—and everything in it—for the very first time.

There are three stages of a man's life: he believes in Santa Claus, he doesn't believe in Santa Claus, he is Santa Claus.

So I ask you: how can people not believe in magic? How can people not believe in themselves?

The world is absolutely full of elves—and you are one of them!

OF "HALLO-GIVING-MAS," HEROES, AND THE NORTH POLE

Christmas is over and business is business.

—FRANKLIN PIERCE ADAMS

About four hundred and fifty miles north of Greenland, at the very top of the Earth's axis, laced by the cold, gray waters of the Arctic Ocean, is a desolate place of drifting ice and snow known as the North Pole.

This is, of course, the geographic North Pole—not to be confused with the magnetic North Pole. Compass needles point to the magnetic North Pole, which is actually just as well. There has recently been a steady flow of nuclear submarines, jet planes, weather balloons, and *National Geographic* photographers in and out of that area. I say just as well because it's much better to have all that traffic moving through the magnetic North Pole. This is because Santa Claus and his elves live in the geographic North Pole where, believe me, the fewer interruptions there are the better our lives are going to be.

Considering what you know (or most probably don't know about the place), the obvious question becomes: why did Santa Claus ever choose to settle on a piece of real estate as far away and as desolate as the North Pole? Granted, it is the top of the world, but—on the other hand—you certainly don't read about people retiring to the North Pole, do you? Everyone heads south to Miami where it's warm. How many families have you ever known who've loaded up the station wagon for a vacation to the North Pole? Again, they usually head to Disneyland, where it's almost always warm.

The simple and unadorned truth is that most of the people who've ever visited the North Pole never actually decided to go there themselves. They were sent—and most of the ones who actually did make an individual decision to go did it simply because they couldn't come up with anything else better to do with their time. (For Robert Peary and Matthew Henson, it was a matter of wanting to take their sled dogs for a very long walk.)

We may as well be bottom line here. Nobody's ever won a trip for two to the North Pole on any television game show. If you want a terrific laugh, get the Club Med folks on the phone and ask about their resort location closest to the geographic North Pole! Try thumbing through the pages of any real estate magazine to see what's listed under North Pole condominium opportunities!

Did you know that an elf is required to work for only two days out of an entire year? It's the truth! However, considering that a single day at the North Pole is six months long, that's really not saying one whole heck of a lot, now is it?

I think I've made my point. The North Pole is a vast, endless, enormous, and whopping expanse of frigid nothing—unless, of course, you count the ice, wind, and snow. Nobody lives at the North Pole! Nobody ever really goes there—at least not on their own accord. So why—why in the name of Christmas—did Santa Claus ever in his right mind choose the North Pole as home?

The answer is—(are you ready for this?)—he didn't! Do you actually think, given a choice, he would've selected the geographic North Pole as the number one place he wanted to call mi casa? Even national hockey teams have turned the North Pole down! (If you can't tell where the ice ends, players are always out-of-bounds!)

Now, if Santa Claus didn't choose the North Pole for himself, who did? Who made the decision to take this poor man, beloved by millions of people the world over, and stick him—along with the rest of us, mind you—at the top of the blooming world in the middle of a frozen nothing?

You did. That's right. Don't look so surprised. The shoe fits, Cinderella! You made the decision. By *you* I naturally mean *you humans*. And, please excuse me, but I've been dying to ask you one question:

What is it with you people?

(Is this any way to show affection?)

For years now, you've gone off on incredibly wild tangents, glibly deciding amongst yourselves that we have nothing better to do than to live at the North Pole, occupying ourselves (not to mention our valuable time) with the most asinine activities.

Give us a break, folks! This may come as a huge shock to some of you, but elves don't march around all day singing catchy little tunes like the Oompa Loompas did in *Willie Wonka's Chocolate Factory*. (Trust me on this.) It's high time you people faced up to a few facts about yourselves and how you treat your heroes.

Did you know that there's a town in Spencer County, Indiana—just thirty-eight miles from Evansville—called Santa Claus? Well, there is. Every year the post office in Santa Claus re-mails more than one million pieces of Christmas letters just so they can go out with a Santa Claus postmark on 'em.

On the surface, this may seem like an absolutely delightful thing for a town to do—re-stamp envelopes so people can't say they never got a letter from Santa Claus. But think about this for a moment. If you humans have long-since decided that Santa Claus lives at the North Pole, why are you sending one million pieces of Christmas mail to the state of Indiana?

And just in case you're thinking that the dear citizens of Santa Claus incorporated their little town for the express purpose of handling this annual deluge of Christmas mail, let me put your minds to rest. The town was named Santa Claus because the name Santa Fe had already been taken!

The name Santa Claus was only a desperate second choice, for which, no doubt, some Santa Clausians (most especially the town's unfortunate postmaster) have good reason to rue.

Don't get me wrong. Heaven knows what we'd do at the North Pole with a million more pieces of mail—along with everything else we have to do! It's just that you know where we live! Indiana is a very fine state, but it's not home sweet home for Santa Claus and his merry little band of elves. No. We're freezing our keisters off up at the North Pole because you stuck us here! Actually, a man named George P. Webster was the first person to give everyone the idea when he published a cute little poem in 1869 titled "Santa Claus and His Works." Webster wrote that Santa Claus's home was "near the North Pole, in the ice and snow," and not one human being thought to ask if Webster had been enjoying one or two alcoholic beverages before he sat down to put pen to paper. It was therefore unanimously decided that the boss would absolutely adore some choice real estate smack dab in the center of the geographical North Pole. Yet when it honestly comes down to it, you don't really believe it yourselves—do you?

Now, why is that? Well, let me simply suggest that the geographical North Pole, for all its fictitious allure, is not a place you would have chosen for yourselves. On the other hand, it's a wonderful place to which you relegate one of your greatest heroes. I'm even going to go a step farther and suggest that you may want to consider the occasional and somewhat sadistic side of your natures in having agreed to this choice in the first place.

First of all, you chose someone truly worthy of emulation … someone whose unselfishness and sense of brotherhood are annually paraded about as an example worthy of following every single day of the year.

Then, almost immediately, you started confusing everything! To begin with, Halloween merchandise is hardly out on corner drugstore shelves before those orange, plastic Jack-o'-lanterns are made to share counter space with boxes of Christmas cards, ornaments, and strings of computerized, blinking lights. Ever tried shopping for your Thanksgiving turkey while the supermarket's taped music du jour happens to be "It's Beginning To Look a Lot Like Christmas?" And you people actually wonder why you always feel so rushed during the holidays?

Personally … and I know I'm digressing here, but … I think you should give yourselves a break. As long as you're rushing through everything, why not combine all three holidays into one. Call it Hallo-giving-mas and just get it over with as soon as humanly possible—with a minimum amount of merchandising headaches, food preparation, mandatory relatives, crowded airports, and all the resulting depression!

Of course you'll never do it. You'll never do it because it's too logical. And logical behavior, I'm afraid, has never been your human forte. No. You'd still prefer three round-trips to the attic (one for the Halloween decorations, one for the Thanksgiving decorations, and one for the Christmas decorations) when, instead, you could be making a single round trip to the attic for a single box of Hallo-giving-mas decorations. And what's more, you could keep them on display in your home for three full months! Never happen though. Too logical.

Stay with me. I'm working around to my original point about heroes and the North Pole.

Finally, the Christmas holidays arrive—the third installment in this annual bacchanal of rapid-fire holidays and a classic example of how you treat heroes. Because, along with this particular holiday, come the Santa Clauses! (Yes, I used the plural!) Wooden, metal, plastic—small, medium, large. You just name it, and there's a Santa Claus clone to fit the bill. He's everywhere! And he's doing everything from selling used cars on television to parachuting into shopping center parking lots! He's shivering on almost every street corner, clanging that shrill and irritating little hand bell.

And just to add insult to injury, you've even got Santa coming after people with an axe in a movie called *Silent Night, Deadly Night*. Now this is absolutely beyond the pale! (*National Enquirer* hasn't taken him on yet, but I'm convinced it's only a matter of time.)

Still, no matter how you market, package, or present him, the fact remains that it's all done for one reason. The man is famous! He's a perfect role model, a VIP, a star, a legend—a genuine, cultural icon. He's even bigger than Elvis! In short—what we've got here is a bona-fide hero! And that's exactly why you stuck him in the North Pole.

You don't honestly want to live with your role models on a daily basis. You only seem to be able to deal with them from afar. (And the North Pole is about as far afar as you can get!) What's more, you don't seem to handle your heroes too well in long doses. Even Santa Claus is only trotted out once a year!

Granted, you can often snap the littles into line by reminding them that "he's making a list and checking it twice." There were actually times when Santa Claus was referred to as Aschen Klaus, which means Ash Nicholas, because biggles thought that a few littles should think of Santa, aside from bringing toys, as being someone who also carried around a sack of ashes and a bundle of switches. But think about it. How many naughty littles have you ever really known who actually got switches or lumps of coal on Christmas morning? I don't think anyone honestly believes that this infamous list, supposedly kept by Santa, really amounts to a hill of beans. Naughty or nice, everybody's included in Christmas. Always! That's just the way the boss operates.

And that's also why it's never a good idea to say to someone who's not being particularly nice, "You'll be sorry on Christmas morning!" They never are. Most probably, they never will be. That's because Christmas presents were never intended to be part of some grand reward system for being nice. I mean, nice certainly helps, but it's not the sole determining factor. Beside, we're talking about Christmas, not the Spanish Inquisition.

The ancient Romans were actually the first ones to start the whole practice of exchanging presents. Every December they celebrated a holiday called Saturnalia. During this particular time, everyone gave each other good-luck presents of fruit, pastry, sometimes even gold. But that was it! These gifts weren't rewards for being nice. They were merely ways of saying good luck in the attempt to be. Much more realistic, if you ask me. In a strange sort of way, you human beings today are making heroism (as well as Christmas itself) almost unattainable. You're making it a matter of perfection—and that's never been the idea at all. For instance, suppose it was a rule that only people who'd been nice all year long were the ones who got presents on Christmas morning. Beside someone like Mother Teresa, who do you know who'd even have a reason to glance under the tree?

Regardless of what television commercials tell you, (and the average American sees or hears five hundred sixty advertisements every day!) Christmas is not a perfect time celebrated by perfect people. The house is not always spotlessly clean, and the turkey is not always cooked to absolute perfection. The honest truth is that, for most people, Christmas is a rushed and harried time of cooking, cleaning, wrapping presents, fielding relatives, fighting crowds in shopping malls, spending money, and meeting hundreds of deadlines. That's not Merry Christmas; that's Merry Crisis Management!

Well, please take some advice from an elf who knows. Don't worry about being perfect. Never going to happen anyway! Remember what Benjamin Franklin wrote in *Poor Richard's Almanac*: "Who is wise? He that learns from every One. Who is powerful? He that governs his Passions. Who is rich? He that is content. Who is that? Nobody." At the

North Pole, we'd call this "low elf esteem." Besides, no one ever gets penalized for not being perfect at Christmas! (In fact, it actually works in reverse most of the time.) The less perfect you are, the better holiday season you might possibly expect. Need an example? All right, here you are: Ebenezer Scrooge. Remember him? He was the stingiest, meanest man in town—not at all the type of person you'd describe as a candidate for receiving Christmas gifts from anyone.

So what happens to this stingy old miser in *A Christmas Carol?* Everybody in the book spends the major portion of the story being unbelievably nice to him! And this is a man who declares that any idiot celebrating Christmas should be "boiled in his own Christmas pudding and buried with a stake of holly through his heart." He does everything but spit into people's faces, and still he gets visited by wonderful apparitions, learns to fly, drinks from the wine of human kindness, among other absolutely splendid things. And all for what? For being absolutely, completely, and unequivocally mean!

The moral here is that simply being nice is definitely not a prerequisite for being rewarded on Christmas morning. Whatever happened to being nice simply because it was the decent thing to do? Life doesn't shape itself to fit into our personal value system or time schedule.

It may very well be unwise to teach your littles that they are always going to be rewarded by other people for being nice. I think you know that human beings often have a tendency to react in a completely opposite manner. Good King Wenceslas—the guy with a Christmas carol named after him—was a tenth-century Bohemian nobleman (Duke of Borivoy) who lived to be only twenty-six years old. He didn't live to be any older than that because his mother and twin brother killed him. And just to add insult to injury, they did him in while the poor man was attending a church service—a man so nice that his first name was Good! Go figure!

On the other hand, only being nice to nice people is much too easy—like preaching to the choir. There's a famous joke from the North Pole: "Why did the elf cross the road?" Answer? "In order to see both sides!" So, go on! Give yourself a challenge! Take a Scrooge to lunch! Better yet, give a Scrooge a hug. Won't cost you a dime. And the results may absolutely astound you … one way or the other. So what if you don't succeed the first time out? Hang in there! Stay with it! Tenacity has its virtues.

Do you remember the famous impressionist painter Claude Monet? He painted more than three hundred pictures of the same lily pads in the same pond in his same backyard! Why? He stayed with the subject until he felt he'd gotten it right. Not perfect, just … right. Well, I, for one, would like to say: "Way to go, Claude!"

The Times Mirror Center did a study entitled "The Age of Indifference." Its subject was "young Americans and how they view the news." The title of the study wasn't just pulled out of thin air. This report concluded that your young Americans know less and care less about the news than any other generation of Americans in the last fifty years!

Asked about career goals, almost none of those surveyed chose the helping occupations that they also rated highest in moral value. Asked for one wish, nearly every boy chose money. And the dreams of your young people? "Five million dollars and a day at the mall!"

Another study concluded that 70 percent of Americans believe that their country has no living heroes. About the same number say that your children have no role models. Some littles are even afraid of Santa Claus! (We call them "Claustrophobics.") So—there you are. Still, I can't help but wonder if you people have been looking in the right places.

Most heroes are simply ordinary people placed in extraordinary situations. This premise accepted, every single human being can look forward to the opportunity of being a hero at one time or another. Because at some point in your life, the odds are that you will find yourself in an extraordinary situation. It will have nothing to do with the degree of perfection you have or haven't attained.

Most probably it will be a matter of simply keeping your wits about you and, in a split second, determining a rational and civilized course of action. Stated even more plainly, a hero is often an individual who sees something good that needs to be done ... and does it. Again, this is not a matter of perfection. It's a matter of doing what is right. This is why it's extremely important that you know why heroes are heroes.

In Crystal City, Texas, there's a six-foot high stone monument dedicated to the comic-strip character Popeye. Now, you ask any little who Popeye is, and they'll tell you he's the one who eats his spinach. But Popeye the Sailor is not a hero because he eats his spinach. He is a hero because, generally, he recognizes what needs to be done and does it. Spinach just helps him get the job done more quickly. (I do hope that's a relief to those of you who have always hated spinach and felt so much guilt all these many years.)

This hero concept is one of the reasons you've relegated the boss (along with the rest of us) to the North Pole. You've somehow gotten this crazy idea that Santa Claus is going to be disappointed with your lack of perfection if you allow him any closer. Of course, I have to admit that I can hardly fault you in this case. As I said before, you were raised to think he was keeping that infamous list—and watching you all the time—just waiting for you to make a mistake. When you get right down to it, your concept of Santa Claus has been that he's more of a private detective than the true spirit of Christmas.

That's because Santa Claus has already been defined for most people—and they simply accept the definition as presented. And to those of you who are scared stiff at the thought of even attempting to change the image of Santa Claus, let me remind you that subtle alterations have already been going on for years! For instance, in Bavaria, St. Nicholas was once considered to be only a message runner. That is to say the Bavarians believed the boss's job was simply to take children's Christmas requests up to heaven. That was it. Bavarians believed it was a representative of the infant Jesus who actually delivered the gifts to the world on Christmas

Eve. This heavenly representative was known in Bavaria as Liebes Christkind, or Dear Christ Child. When this tradition finally reached America, it went through several changes. Christkind became Kriss Kringle. And the rest, as they say, is happy holiday history.

In Germany, St. Nicholas is known as Weinachtsmann, which literally means "Christmas man." In Russia, he's known as Father Frost. In France, he's Pere Noel. In England, they call him Father Christmas, and the list goes on.

The main thing to remember is that joy, happiness, and contentment (and Santa Claus) are very personal things. We define them for ourselves through an ongoing process of internalization and re-examination. This is because life's truest meaning always comes from within—and only after we begin to focus on that internal vision. Just as our own concepts of happiness and contentment may change with time, so may our internal vision (and definition) of Santa Claus.

Well, isn't it perhaps time to let go of a few things—to discard some of those old images of who you think the boss is and of just how he does what he does? At the very least, isn't this a wonderful opportunity to re-think and re-examine? This doesn't mean that you have to deny the little inside of you in the process—or discard a single warm memory of your past experience. You're going to happily discover that the little inside of you becomes a lot healthier when the weight of so much guilt doesn't have to be lugged around anymore. In fact, re-examining your entire concept of what and who all of your heroes are might be a very healthy thing to do. Just remember that demanding perfection of all your heroes is perfectly acceptable—so long as all of your heroes are saints. You'll be able to better accept the absence of perfection in some of your closer heroes when you're able to accept and forgive the lack of perfection in yourself.

Leo Tolstoy said, "The highest purpose of art is to make people good by choice." Paraphrased, that's a fine description of Santa's purpose in the world as well. Good by choice—not by guilt. There's enough in this world humans should feel guilty about.

Being less than perfect—particularly during the Christmas season—is just not one of them.

A DICKENS OF A DAY!

A Christmas family party! We know nothing in nature more delightful! There seems a magic in the very name of Christmas.

—CHARLES DICKENS

The weather in Manchester, England, can sometimes seem especially cold and bleak. The particular October day that begins this story was definitely one of those times! Winter was in the air. The merciless wind seemed unusually harsh and damp. People trudged up and down the streets with heads bowed against the bitterness of it. No one smiled. At least the sun was still up. That was one consolation. Of course, you couldn't really see it through the heavy layer of gray clouds. Still, just knowing it was there seemed to help … a little.

When night finally came to this particular city, on this particular day, the cheeriness of what little daylight there had been faded completely from the sky. The streets emptied quickly as the people of Manchester hurried home without a sound. When, at last, the icy darkness had wrapped itself around the quiet streets and buildings of the town, the whole world seemed to take a deep, collective breath before sinking into a long and lingering depression. All together. All at once.

Now, there was an undeniable ray of hope ahead—something to look forward to—if people had only realized it. Christmas was coming, and, as everyone knows, Christmas is the happiest day of the year. Yet, judging by the dreariness of the day, the empty streets and the silence of that cold, lonely night, you would hardly have known it. But then, that was probably because no one hardly did know it. You see, the year was 1843, and a few things we take for granted now were very, very different then.

A Christmas card or two might have reminded a few people to cheer up a bit. But no one ran to the mailbox to see who might have sent them one. There wasn't much need to do so. Christmas cards weren't introduced to the world until 1846. That meant that on this particular evening in Manchester, England, Christmas cards (and all the wonderful cheer that might have come along with them) were still three long years away!

Even if there had been Christmas cards in 1843, they wouldn't have changed the fact that there still wasn't very much Christmas to look forward to anyway!

It might be hard for you to imagine, but this was a time when December 25th was a hardly noticed, one-day holiday. It came and went without much fanfare at all. Littles might hope to get a couple of presents apiece, of course, but that was about it. On Christmas day, most biggles simply sat around the house and read—which, when you got down to it, wasn't so very different from what they did almost every other day of the year. It's very safe to say that if anyone thought about Christmas at all in 1843, the word *festive* wasn't the first thing to pop into their minds. But the shocking fact that Christmas came and went without too much notice didn't really affect people one way or the other. After all, they had no way of knowing what they were missing!

If something extra special hadn't happened, we'd probably all still be "celebrating" Christmas just this very same way—which is to say, we wouldn't be celebrating Christmas very much at all!

The world had just settled in for that long, cold October evening when the sound of footsteps broke the empty silence. A lone man, shielded against the weather by top hat, warm scarf, and long cloak, came into view. Making his solitary way along the deserted streets of the town, he seemed wrapped as much in deep thought as he was by that long, warm cloak against the evening's chill.

Occasionally he would pause before the glow of a lighted window to gaze inside. His eyes would carefully absorb the typical scene within—a family gathered around the evening fire, a small child playing idly with a favorite toy, someone silently reading by candle light. For a moment he would take in all he saw. Then, with a sigh and a shrug, he would eventually resume his quiet and lonesome promenade.

He appeared to be the only living soul foolish enough to venture outside that evening. And yet, despite the season's icy chill and the solitary nature of his journey, he seemed quite content in having the night all to himself.

He was just passing through a pool of light cast by the occasional, friendly blaze of a street lamp when a man's soft voice interrupted his thoughts.

"Evening, sir."

A bit startled, the man in the top hat and long cloak paused to peer into the darkness just beyond the light.

"Good evening, yourself," was his reply.

Another gentleman, also warmly dressed against the evening's chill, stepped into the street lamp's friendly glow.

"Well!" said the man in top hat and cloak, "I hardly expected to find anyone else on the streets tonight."

"Yes, I know," the stranger replied with a friendly smile.

For a moment the two men simply gazed at each other in comfortable silence. Then the stranger spoke again.

"You're Mr. Charles Dickens, aren't you?" he asked.

The man in top hat and cloak smiled. "I am," he answered.

"I've read your work," continued the stranger, "You've quite a talent as a writer."

Charles Dickens, the man in the top hat and cloak, was thirty-one years old. And on this particular evening in Manchester, England, he had already achieved extraordinary status as a writer. His books were beginning to be read and loved the world over. By this time in his career, he had completed *Oliver Twist*, *Nicholas Nickleby*, and *The Old Curiosity Shop*, among others. Yet he was still, as they say, "poised on the threshold of greatness."

"I've certainly no wish to intrude," the stranger continued, "but I see you're walking alone. Would you care for some
company?"

Dickens considered for a moment. Usually on these solitary jaunts, he preferred to be by himself. But something in
the stranger's voice and smile softened his resolve.

"As a matter of fact," he said, "I'd very much appreciate
some company this evening, Mister …?"

"Nicholas," replied the stranger.

"Well, Mr. Nicholas," the great author said with a sigh,
"you and I seem to be the only two people brave enough to
stir abroad on a night like this. That being the case, I believe
we'd be only prudent to follow the adage which advises that
misery not only needs, but rather enjoys company."

And that's the way they met—Charles and Nicholas—on
a cold and dreary October evening in Manchester, England,
under the warm glow of a street lamp. And what followed
was one of those pivotal, but unrecorded moments in history,
when the course of human thought is irrevocably altered due
to a passing, and perhaps even unintended, act or deed.

They walked together for hours, these two men, for probably twenty miles—up and down the deserted streets of an
empty city. And they spoke of things—important things—
thoughts that shape the life of a man, dreams that tend to
forge a soul destined for greatness.

The two men had walked silently abreast for a while
when Nicholas again broke the silence. "Mr. Dickens, I hope

you don't mind me saying so," he began, "but you seem somehow troubled this evening. May I ask why?"

"Is it that obvious?" Dickens asked, adjusting the collar of his long cloak to better shield himself from the wind. Nicholas simply kept silent pace with his new-found companion.

"As it so happens, I am troubled," Dickens confessed, "I feel as if the cares of the entire world were weighing down upon me tonight."

"Quite a burden," Nicholas said softly, "The cares of the entire world! I hope you have strong shoulders, sir."

"It's not shoulders I need!" snapped Dickens. "It's making a difference that's vital. And I must confess to you that, as a writer, I am, this evening, feeling somewhat inadequate to the task."

"What sort of difference do you wish to make?" asked Nicholas.

Dickens stopped walking. He didn't say anything for a moment but only stared straight into the darkness ahead. Suddenly he turned to Nicholas with a new sense of purpose.

"I've recently come from London," he explained, "From Field Lane, as a matter of fact, a rather ragged charity school for children in Saffron Hill."

"Ah, yes." Nicholas sighed. "I happen to know it well."

"Then you also must know what a deplorable place it is," Dickens continued with growing enthusiasm, "Well meaning, but totally inadequate."

"Yes," Nicholas replied, "as a matter of fact, I do know."

Again there was another thoughtful silence as the two men continued together down the quiet street.

"If I'm not mistaken," Nicholas began again, "isn't Field Lane located on the very same spot Fagin occupied in *Oliver Twist*?"

Dickens stopped in his tracks and turned to face his walking companion. Again, he couldn't help but smile. "You have a rather good memory for details," Dickens observed wryly.

"So I've been told." Nicholas chuckled. "In this case, however, I much prefer to think of it as merely having the good sense to recognize a brilliant writer ... when I read one."

Another moment slipped quietly by until the silence was broken again by Nicholas. "You really do want to change the world, don't you?" he asked, placing a hand on his new friend's shoulder. The gleam in the eyes of Charles Dickens was all the answer he needed. "In that case," Nicholas concluded, "why don't you get on with it?"

Charles Dickens gazed intently at the man before him and offered a reply that has excused (and haunted) mankind's apathy for ages past ... and ages yet to come.

"What difference can I possibly make?" he implored. "I'm only one man. One man against an apathetic world!" Dickens shoved his hands into the pockets of his long cloak and fretfully paced back and forth for a moment.

"Do you realize," he finally continued, "that in our country today only one child out of three attends even a rudimentary school? Thousands of children never attend school at all! And it's not simply that they can't afford it. They're not allowed to afford it!"

"Yes, I know," Nicholas replied evenly, "and that is why I still ask. When do you plan to get on with changing things for the better?"

Dickens, in one grand gesture of helplessness, threw back his head and flung his arms wide. "For God's sake, man!" he cried in his best orator's voice, "I write books! I entertain the masses for a few short hours. At best, if I occupy their minds at all, it is to direct their attention away from the cares and problems of the world. No one wishes to see the world as it truly is! They only want to see what they imagine it to be!"

"I beg your pardon then," Nicholas replied with just a tinge of firmness in his voice, "I must have been mistaken. I was under the impression that I was addressing the author of *Oliver Twist*—a novel that, as I recall, dealt quite remarkably with the injustices society all too often inflicts upon the children of this world. I believed you to be the man who used the power of his creative gifts to help raise the level of that same society's collective consciousness. I imagined you to be the sort of man who still might wish to do much more … if he could. You are a writer. You know the power of the written word. What has changed your mind?"

The question brought Dickens to a standstill. For a moment, he could only stare blankly into the eyes of his companion. Nicholas returned the gaze with a comfortable and disarming smile. Finally, the great author spoke.

"My present situation," he said in soft reply, "is what has changed my mind."

"In what way?" asked Nicholas.

Dickens sighed deeply and began again. "You say I have talent as a writer and that my talent has the power to change the lives of others ... to make the world a better place for the rest of humanity? That very well may be. But tell me, sir, what good is that to me when I, myself, am hard pressed to provide for the basic needs of my own family? They cannot clothe themselves in my talent. They cannot be housed in it. You do not set talent on the table for an evening meal. The simple truth is that I am desperate for money. I have debts, you see ... financial obligations to my family, my publisher, my creditors. Setting down the truth on paper is a great satisfaction to my soul. That is its value to me. But if the truth cannot also put meat upon my table, what is it finally worth? That is why I no longer sit at my desk, pen in hand, asking my soul if what I am writing is true. Now I merely ask myself if what I am writing will sell."

If silence has ever seemed deafening, it seemed so in that one moment. Even in the dim glow of that distant street lamp, Nicholas could plainly see the grief in Dickens's eyes.

"May I ask you a question?" said Nicholas finally. Dickens did not reply. "If one day, while walking along the Thames, you were to see a child accidentally fall into the water, what would you do?"

The question immediately returned Dickens's gaze to Nicholas.

"Would you," Nicholas continued, "leap into the water to try and save that child? Or would you pause to consider what the worth of the deed might be to you? Would you need, as well, a moment to consider the value of your actions?"

Nicholas let the unanswered questions hang for a time in the icy silence of the night. Dickens stood ramrod straight, boring into him with blazing eyes.

"Perhaps," Nicholas went on, "you would also need a moment more to consider the possible effects of your deed upon the lives of your family. After all, what if, in the attempt to save that child, you were to lose your own life? And surely you would have to consider how your publisher or creditors would ever be repaid. And so when you had asked yourself all these questions ... after you had taken pause to carefully compare the worth of the deed against its value ... and only when your soul was quite satisfied with the answers ... would you then try to save that drowning child?"

Dickens remained frozen before Nicholas for a moment or two. Then ... all at once ... the great author's chest rose, fell, and actually seemed to shudder beneath the weight of some enormous and unspeakable emotion.

"I suggest to you," Nicholas concluded with quiet gentleness, "that at this very moment, thousands of the world's children are drowning in a great river of neglect, loneliness, and despair. And, for reasons that escape our poor powers of human comprehension, God has chosen to place you, my good sir, on the riverbank. Now you may, if you so choose, take the luxury of time for consideration. I only hope you find your answers before the cries of those children have been silenced forever. After all, answers are easy, Mr. Dickens. Only the questions are hard."

A very wise person once said that the greatest moments in our lives happen during the silences. So it was, that in the ensuing silence of that cold October night, Charles Dickens, the greatest author of his time—quietly and freely—wept.

Every mystery of the world has a solution. All of life's great questions were answered long before we ever even began to consider them. Each answer—each solution—lies, simply hidden, in the hearts of man. They have been within us from the beginning of time. All too frequently, however, we lose the discovery of truth to the self-imposed complexity of our desperate search to find it. In our long and arduous journeys to reach paradise, we awake to discover, often too late, that we have already passed through it many times. The real quest of the human soul has never been to find the right answers. The true quest has always been to simply determine whether we were ever asking the right questions.

In that instant of absolute clarity, when this marvelous realization swept over Dickens, he was immediately and completely transformed. He wept, yes. But he wept for joy! He felt at once the wonderful release from the terrible bondage of too many excuses and too much rationalization. In only one more remarkable moment, his tears gave way to laughter. Happy, uncontrollable, side-splitting laughter! Nicholas laughed too. They both laughed together! They laughed until their sides ached and they were out of breath.

When they could laugh no longer, the two men, arm in arm, joyously resumed their nightlong walk through the dark streets of Manchester. For Dickens, now so miraculously transformed, the night seemed to become fresh and new as well, taking on a special aura all its own—the radiance of which reached down into the inner most depths of his soul, illuminating his entire being with the lustrous light of hope.

The author, grasping a newfound joy in this fresh sense of purpose, became exuberant. His feelings and emotions, held inside for so long, came pouring out like a flood. He began to tell Nicholas all about his life—of his childhood partially spent on London's Bayham Street; of his crippled son, Tiny Fred, so named for Dickens's own brother who was only two years old when their family had moved to England's great capital city. As each long-buried recollection surfaced, Dickens would eagerly describe that memory's particular story to Nicholas. With wonderfully animated gestures, he captured and unfolded tale after tale, assuming, with a master storyteller's practiced skill, this or that marvelous character from his past. As they walked, even his footsteps on the cobblestones seemed to become increasingly brisk and light. Five miles turned to ten, and ten miles turned to twenty before the night was spent. And all during their time together, Nicholas stayed close by his side, listening in rapt attention as the great author healed his heart through the simple magic of his own remembrances.

Only when Dickens finally lapsed into happy silence did Nicholas dare to speak again. When he finally did, he began slowly and deliberately—not wishing to break the evening's fresh spell.

"Charles," he said with newfound familiarity, "when you write again, why not set down these stories you've just shared with me. Why not write about the things you know and feel so deeply?"

Dickens, pausing to draw a breath, considered his friend's proposal.

"My stories?" he said aloud, repeating the idea to himself.

"Of course!" Nicholas urged with a smile. "Why not?"

Only then, for the first time since Dickens began to laugh earlier in the evening, did the two men stop walking. The author turned to face Nicholas once more.

"You've not really been searching for the truth, Charles," Nicholas confided, "You've simply been searching for yourself—for the child you used to be! You've been seeking a way to go back—to heal the hurt you knew. For a time you were lost. But tonight you found the way! I believe the door to the past and all of its priceless wonders has been opened to you. Life is short, and this doesn't happen for everyone. So please don't stand too long on the threshold! Go in. Go back to what you were—to that little boy with all his hurts, his hopes, and his wonderful dreams. You'll find him there. He's been waiting for you."

"And then what?" Dickens probed, "What do I do then?"

Nicholas patted his friend's shoulder before starting off into the night.

"You're a writer!" he called out over his shoulder. "What do you think you do?"

"But how?" Dickens pleaded, "Where do I begin?"

"You'll think of something!" Nicholas called, waving a cheerful good-bye to his friend as he sauntered away. "If it's any help to you at all, Christmas is just around the corner!"

"That it is!" Dickens called out, "The merriest Christmas ever!"

Nicholas paused briefly and, cocking an eyebrow, added with a departing smile, "Wouldn't be at all surprised. Oh! And that reminds me, Charles ... heard any good Christmas carols lately?"

In another second, Nicholas had vanished—disappearing completely into the pre-dawn darkness as suddenly as he had appeared. He left the rejuvenated author practically riveted to his spot on the sidewalk, a quizzical look spreading across his face as the first rays of sunlight began to streak the clear skies over Manchester, England.

Charles Dickens's book, *A Christmas Carol*, published by Chapman and Hall solely on the basis of a commission, appeared in London bookstores on Christmas day, 1843. It had taken the author only a little over six weeks to compose the entire story! Bound in red cloth, with a beautiful gilt design on the cover, it sold six thousand copies the first day alone! It became one of the most beloved stories in the English language—one of the greatest books of all time! The very first stage adaptation of *A Christmas Carol* premiered in 1844—only a year after the book was published. To date, at least forty film versions, dozens of recordings, and several television adaptations have celebrated the transformation of the mean-spirited old miser whose confrontation with the past and future transforms him, in a single night, into a new person.

The original manuscript of the book was carefully preserved and, after many wanderings, is now part of the Pierpont Morgan Library in New York, where it is exhibited to thousands of people every year.

Robert Seymour, the great Dickens biographer, once suggested that Charles Dickens actually invented Christmas. It isn't true, of course, and everyone knows it. It is safe to say, however, that Dickens's little book did help to revive the celebration of Christmas—not only in England but throughout the entire world. He achieved this miracle by simply taking his readers back to the child within themselves. He reminds us all, in a unique and loving way, that the true spirit of Christmas is actually a shared sense of childhood—a special time "of active usefulness, perseverance, cheerful discharge of duty, kindness and forbearance"—a time of personal recommitment to the dreams we hold so dearly within our hearts, the universal desire for true and lasting peace on earth, goodwill toward men. Dickens's wonderful book gave those dreams a voice and still reminds us that they are attainable after all.

And yet, more than the beautiful story itself, the unique quality of his personal passion for the subject is what gave the book its true and lasting greatness. Because, in the writing of *A Christmas Carol*, it was as if Dickens—through the character of Ebenezer Scrooge—actually returned to his own child-hood and relived it. In doing so, he swept his readers along. His journey—his healing—became theirs as well. Long before we ever derived a clinical name for the process, before we even began to understand its therapeutic value, Dickens already knew, instinctively, that such spiritual journeys are as much a part of life and growth (and the holiday season) as breath itself.

In fact, he explains it very well in his own words when he writes:

> There are people who will tell you that Christmas is not to them what it used to be; that each succeeding Christmas has found some cherished hope, or happy prospect, of the year before, dimmed or passed away; that the present only serves to remind them of reduced circumstances and straitened incomes—of the feasts they once bestowed on hollow friends, and of the cold looks that meet them now, in adversity and misfortune. Never heed such dismal reminiscences. There are few men who have lived long enough in the world, who cannot call up such thoughts any day in the year. Then do not select the merriest of the three hundred and sixty-five for your doleful recollections, but draw your chair nearer the blazing fire—fill the glass and send 'round the song—and if your room be smaller than it

was a dozen years ago, or if your glass be filled with reeking punch, instead of sparkling wine, put a good face on the matter, and empty it off-hand, and fill another, and troll off the old ditty you used to sing, and thank God it's no worse ...

Who can be insensible to the outpourings of good feeling, and the honest interchange of affectionate attachment which abound at this season of the year. A Christmas family party! We know nothing in nature more delightful! There seems a magic in the very name of Christmas.

In the writing of *A Christmas Carol*, Charles Dickens used everything his memory could possibly reach back to touch! The Dickens family home on Bayham Street became the small terraced house inhabited by the Cratchit family. His own brother, Tiny Fred, became the story's Tiny Tim. Scrooge's obsession with material wealth had been his own. As Dickens had purged it in his own life, so Scrooge did in his story. It wasn't by accident that Scrooge's extraordinary journey back into his past began with the appearance of a Christmas spirit.

And, for the rest of his days, Charles Dickens knew there was more to that part of the story than most people ever imagined.

ALL I WANT FOR CHRISTMAS

Most all the time, the whole year round, there ain't no flies
on me, but jest 'fore Christmas I'm as good as I kin be!

—EUGENE FIELD

It's not often that Santa Claus makes a mistake. When he
does, it's usually an unqualified doozy! For instance, he
never thought Hula-Hoops were going to be so popular.
(Of course, that may be due to the fact that the boss could
hardly fit one of them around his middle.) And pet rocks? He
couldn't believe how well they went over! I mean, after all,
he's predicted most of the world's other fads with astounding
accuracy. That's why it's always such a kicker whenever some
unqualified hit manages to slip by him.

When it does happen, and the boss realizes he's missed
the bull's eye by that old proverbial mile, he paces around the
toyshop, shaking his head and chuckling to himself. Sometimes he'll mutter something like, "A pet rock! A rock! Go
figure that." Of course, we elves always pretend we don't
notice. We try very hard, but it's a losing cause. As surely as

the sun will rise tomorrow, one of us eventually giggles out loud. (Usually me!) Then everybody loses it! The boss laughs at himself harder, louder, and longer than anyone else. (By the way: having one hundred to two hundred belly laughs a day is the equivalent of a high-impact workout, burning off up to five hundred calories.) North Pole company rule: we always have lots of fun—most especially when we make mistakes. It's just not healthy for elves or people to take themselves too seriously all the time.

Now I should make it very clear that those of us who work for the boss aren't in the fad business. Of course, we gear our assembly line toward producing what people ask for, but we're also natural observers of human behavior. We have to be—we're absolutely mesmerized at how you determine what will or won't become a fad in the first place. (It's certainly no secret to elves that Americans comprise only 5 percent of the world's population and yet consume 25 percent of its natural resources! After all, we've read your Christmas wish lists.) Our own personal curiosity aside, fads have an enormous impact on the whole holiday gift-giving process. We produce what people ask for—and people, unfortunately, tend to ask for what's popular with everyone else.

In the vernacular of the marketing world, a fad is anything that's "hot." For something to be considered "hot," it has to be either chic, current, hip, fashionable, trendy, popular, smart, or in vogue. (How about a quarter for every time a salesperson ever said to you, "Everybody's wearing this!")

Anything can become a fad—and I mean anything. Swallowing live goldfish was once very trendy. (This is actually how sushi was first introduced to the American public.) Seeing how many people you could cram into a single telephone booth came next. (This fad developed when all of those people who'd just swallowed live goldfish rushed to the phone to call for medical assistance.)

Conversation used to be "in." Oh, you wouldn't believe how people used to talk with each other! Families, friends, governments, nations—there was a time when everybody communicated with everybody else. Eventually conversation went the way of most fads and just died out. Unfortunately for the world, once that happened, they came up with another fad to take its place. That fad became known as waging war.

Nosegays were once very popular in Elizabethan England. They were small bouquets of aromatic herbs and flowers that women used to carry around all the time. Unlike war, this particular fad had a sensible rationale behind it. Nosegays became popular because bathing wasn't. There was a time when nobody took baths! Bathing simply wasn't "in." So women, out of necessity more than anything else, took to sniffing nosegays whenever some friendly but odorous person got too close for too long.

Of course some women decided not to follow the trend and absolutely refused to carry nosegays. This group of women created another popular fad called "passing out from the unbearable stench." When other women found out they could simply pass out instead of carrying nosegays ... bingo! Women started dropping like flies.

Unfortunately, in the midst of so much passing out and falling down, people eventually forgot one interesting fact about human nature. A good mood has a distinct smell! Absolutely true. Scientists have found that people can judge whether someone is in a positive mood from their body odor alone. Perhaps nosegays were added because of a deep-seated desire that, given a choice, humans would quite naturally wish to encounter someone who is in a good mood. Thus a sweet scent became related to a happy scent—and the rest, as they say, became wonderful news for the personal hygiene industry.

Men, on the other hand, did not adopt the practice of fainting from the smell. After all, somebody had to be there to catch all of the falling women. The unfortunate backlash was that men eventually started a fad of their own and began to label women as "the weaker sex." This, in itself, became a real trendy thing to do. Regrettable, but trendy. If you adopt a fad as a habit, you'd do well to remember one thing: habits are sometimes very hard to break.

Once you start to group fads in categories of gender, you're simply asking for trouble. As I said, fads can become habits before you realize it. For instance, the good Lord gave everybody tear ducts. All of us—people and elves—have the ability to cry. The trouble is, somewhere along the line, it became a fad for women only. Once crying got a feminine gender label, men naturally backed off, counter-acting with that taunting sing-song admonition they occasionally aim at one another: "Cry, baby, cry. Stick your finger in your eye and watch the water fly!" This was a gentle (but masculine) reminder that women had already staked a claim on exhibiting emotion of any kind in public, so it was hands off to men.

Shakespeare said, "What a piece of work is Man!" The boss just says, "Go figure."

This brings us back to fads and how they relate to that vague Christmas-morning disappointment, which has become known as the post-Christmas syndrome.

Somehow you humans always manage to convince yourselves that what you want for Christmas just happens to be what everybody else wants. Imagine that!

Before you rush out to list yourself in the *Guinness Book of Amazing Coincidences*, however, stop long enough to consider a few things. How did you finally decide what it was you wanted—just had to have—under the tree on Christmas morning? Just sort of ... came to you, did it? Out of the blue?

If you believe that, I've got a bridge I think you'd really be interested in buying ... some real estate in northern Siberia, too!

Here's a news flash, folks: The decision about what you want for Christmas is not made independently. The Chinese invented a unique thing known as "water torture." Madison Avenue simply perfected the procedure.

By the time an average American young person reaches the age of sixteen, he or she will already have seen twenty-four thousand hours of television! The only thing your young people will do more than watch television is sleep. Considering you sleep for one third of your lives, you can begin to see where your grasp on reality is actually coming from—and it's not from your heart or your head.

Talking about a fad! Television is definitely "hot"—and quite a habit with you people. Back in 1946, there were only about ten thousand television sets in the entire United States. In only five years, the number had grown to twelve million! Since television offers something for everybody, there was absolutely no gender problem involved. Men can see all the sports they want, and women can weep and wail over all those wonderful soap operas. Television tells you what you want to hear. Problem solved! And let's not forget your littles. Television has something for them too. Saturday cartoons! (Which brings up the question of your human fascination with mutants. What is it with you people and mutants? I know. I know. Go figure.)

There's a price for all this royal entertainment spilling into millions of living rooms every hour of every day. Most fads (and habits, for that matter) do come with a price. In the case of television, the price you pay comes in the form of commercials. (Why do you think it's called commercial television?) Of course, it's finally gotten so bad that you people have started paying money not to see so many commercials. It's called cable television or satellite TV! They've got you coming and going. Either way, you're going to pay for what you get—which brings up the question of whether what you get is really what you want. Then, of course, you have to follow that with—is what you want really what you need?

If you don't know, television will certainly tell you. And how does the advertising industry do that so well? 'Cause it knows all about you. They know, for instance, that women tend to experience their all-time lowest life satisfaction at age thirty-seven whereas men typically experience it at forty-two. So it won't be by chance that people appearing in television commercials for drug-related remedies will be right within those age groups.

By the time you get to be a biggle, you've started to develop a personal scale of values. You define goals and decide how you're going to reach them. (Hopefully this is done before retirement.)

Littles, on the other hand, are still trying to work those things out for themselves. They're just beginning to shape their own system of values, which, hopefully, will take them safely and successfully through the rest of their lives.

Now, in this case, parents are the first line of defense. Your laws make parents legally responsible, so the buck has been squarely placed, in most cases, on at least two sets of shoulders.

The trouble with this setup is that parents just aren't there for their children twenty-four hours every day. On the other hand, a television set never leaves the house. It doesn't have to be in an office every day between the hours of nine and five. It never has to shop for food or have its hair done. It just sits there like a silent beacon in the darkness—waiting for someone with a few hours of spare time. Well, if littles have anything, it appears to be time. When most of your life is still ahead of you, it seems as if you've got all the time in the world.

Once you've got time to spend, you need something to spend it on. Something…convenient. One of the major determining factors as to whether or not a fad becomes a habit is the matter of convenience. That's because humans tend to worship at convenient altars.

If a fad is convenient, it's got a lot better chance of becoming a habit. Television was custom made to fill this requirement. They've made it so convenient you don't even have to get out of your seat to change the channel. (All you have to do is to remember where the heck you put that little remote control clicker thing!)

Next to your incredible fascination with mutants, you've also got this thing about supply and demand. You've really gotten into a snit about having what you want when you want it. Instant gratification. Only now, in case you didn't know, you're into a situation of supply without demand—at least not right away. These days all you really have to do is create the supply. If you do the job right, and make people honestly believe that what you're supplying is the next best thing to sliced bread, it creates the demand all by itself! I mean, you keep telling somebody long enough and convincingly enough that they want something, and pretty soon, they're going to start to believe it. Once they start to believe it, they've got to have it.

You're letting television begin to define your lives, elect your leaders, tell you what to drive, who to hate, who to worship, how to dress, smell, make love—not to mention how to blow people away if they happen not to agree with you. Ever noticed that whenever somebody disagrees with somebody else on television, it's a sure bet the guns and knives are coming out in the very next scene? On a very simplistic level, it does seem to make a lot of sense. I mean, a corpse can't very well disagree with you about anything. No taxing of your intellectual or verbal skills there! But still—doesn't it all seem to you just a trifle extreme? (And, next to mutants and convenience, what is this thing you people have for violence in slow motion?)

Now, don't get me wrong; there are a lot of great things on television. Those advertising guys are smart enough to know that it has to have a few redeeming features. As long as they can slip episodes of *Masterpiece Theatre* and *Sesame Street* into a day's lineup, they're relatively safe from mandatory warning labels, which advise you that "television can be hazardous to your grasp on reality."

Once some people get the idea that television is becoming an educational thing, they get very nervous. Even your elected officials start standing up in the hallowed halls of your nation's capitol, drawling on about how you ought to let the government hold on to your remote controllers for you—and decide what you should or shouldn't see.

If your country happens to have a war going on in some corner of the world, you can bet your last nickel that you're not going to see too much ongoing news about that fact on television. That's because the powers-that-be have long since decided that the miracle of television should be that it takes your mind off of…"things." Much more alluring to watch someone else dance with a star, see who is wearing what at the Oscars, or which person is going to become the biggest loser, bachelor, bachelorette, Jersey wife, chef, or bridezilla of the week. The funniest thing of all? They call it "reality television." The realization will stagger you for a moment, and then you simply have to fall down laughing!

Couldn't happen, you say? I dunno; it's awfully convenient. But then again, you wouldn't have to worry about having to make another decision. It's the price you pay for letting others do your thinking for you. Once you abdicate the responsibility, you're stuck with what you get. Have you ever considered the fact that if apathy is your nation's greatest problem, nobody's going to care that it is a problem?

I'd say it's about time to wake up and smell the ole java.

Okay, so now we've got television and Christmas—or, as they say on Madison Avenue, the dynamic duo. As a potential marketing possibility, this is what's known as a match made in heaven. An advertising agent's dream! It's a cornucopia of supply, demand, instant gratification, and mind alteration all rolled into one locked-and-loaded blitz of holiday advertising, more lovingly recognized as: "Now, a word from our sponsor."

The first cardinal rule of television is: it's not art unless it sells something. Hard to imagine Handel composing *Mes-*

siah while harboring the ever-present knowledge that he was going to have to include periodic musical breaks so somebody could sell a can of dog food, isn't it? Of course, he could've at least consoled himself with the knowledge that not too many people would even be watching a performance of *Messiah* on television anyway. That's because Mr. Handel broke television's second cardinal rule; nothing gets blown up in *Messiah*! There isn't a single car crash or automatic weapon in the entire piece!

So—the holiday season rolls around. Christmas is just around the corner—a time for peace, love, and the quiet gathering of loved ones around the hearth. A time of gentle reflection—of recommitment to world brotherhood and universal understanding.

Try telling that to the two women I once saw taking down two store display counters, a clerk, and four shopping carts during a knock-down-drag-out, hair-pulling battle for possession of the toy department's last remaining Cabbage Patch Doll! Those two mothers obviously hadn't gotten the message. Or, rather, they had been getting a message; it just happened to be the wrong one. They'd been inundated with weeks of commercial television "breaks," which constantly reminded them that their daughters would never find true happiness in life if they didn't find one of those dolls under the tree on Christmas morning. Those two mothers were on a sort of single-minded crusade where "take no prisoners!" had become the battle cry of the shopping day.

A constantly repeated series of televised sound bites and musical jingles had, over a period of several weeks, transformed these two women into a frightening combination of half June Cleaver and half Manchurian Candidate. The scary thing is that they probably hadn't even noticed what was happening to them. You don't start growing hair all over your body and get claws for fingernails, but something akin to a total transformation is definitely at work.

I'm certainly not saying that all of you should start viewing holiday shopping like Lon Chaney Jr. used to view the full moon! But you've all just gotta become a little more aware of what's being pumped into your living rooms during this time of year. Television, turned on in the home for an average of six hours every day, is playing so often in the background that you don't really notice it anymore. It's not there to educate or even entertain. It's just there to keep you company—fill a void. But you've got to understand what sort of subliminal effect it starts to have on everything you think, say, and do.

Here's where it starts to affect what you want as opposed to what you need. For instance, let's say some pricey Madison Avenue advertising agency decides that all of you are absolutely dying to find a gift-wrapped cockroach under your tree on Christmas morning. Ridiculous, you say? Couldn't happen in a million years? Let me remind you of those pet rocks one more time … a rock that you could walk out in your yard or driveway and pick up for free. So don't think the idea of a gift-wrapped cockroach in your Christmas stocking is too far fetched—not by a long shot!

We've all seen it before. While it's more obvious in littles, it also has a way of creeping onto the Christmas morning faces of biggles too. It's a look that comes from a nebulous sort of disappointment. The reason for this vague Christmas morning look of dissatisfaction is that, while they've gotten everything they asked for, they didn't ask for a single thing they honestly needed. They had abdicated their freedom to choose honestly—free from pressure. Television decided for them. It told them what they wanted! They'd been sucked into a sort of holiday junk food feeding frenzy. An hour later it's as though they hadn't eaten a thing all day.

Above all things, don't try to fake good will toward men. You can't do it anyway. People instinctively know when a gesture or a smile isn't genuine. If you're going to go through the motions of being happy, you may as well *be* happy. It takes less energy. Why does rain drop while snow falls? Doesn't matter. Both of them get to where they're going. How you get there is your business. The thing is to get there.

There's a small, hand-carved sign that hangs on the north wall of the Toy Shop—a constant reminder to the elves who spend the greater portion of our time creating the gifts you people give each other. The little sign simply reads: Your time—the greatest gift of all!

Not a bad idea when you stop to think about it. What's the most valuable thing you can possibly give to anyone else? The most valuable thing you possess? Your time. Your life contains a finite number of hours and minutes. When you've used up your allotted amount, that's it. You'd better be ready to smile and close your eyes or wrinkle your brow and whisper, "Rosebud!" Not all the wealth you possess can buy you one additional second. Time is positively precious! What greater gift can you possibly give to anyone than to give the one thing that's most valuable to you? Time shared with our friends and family, especially during special times of the year, is always something we want—what's more, it's always something we need. It's a gift that enriches the giver as much as the receiver. All it costs is—well, you've got to answer that for yourselves. Just remember this: the longer you wait to give it, the less you have left to give. And a lot of your valuable time is usually spent learning this lesson the hard way. If nothing else, maybe I've saved you a bit more of what we never seem to have enough of.

If that's true, then allow me to stake a little claim and advise you to begin to treat your time in this world as the priceless treasure it really is. Never, ever take it for granted—or dare to think that there'll be more of it later on for you or anyone else. And you can't save it up for a later date either. Little Orphan Annie was right; the sun will come out tomorrow. There's just no guarantee you'll still be around to see it. A very wise person once said the only difference between a rut and a grave are their dimensions.

There is no one in this world exactly like you! You're special—one of a kind! Start treating yourself that way. It has nothing to do with self-inflated pride or over-sized ego. It has everything to do with fundamental truth! God put you here to accomplish something. Gandhi said, "Almost everything we do is insignificant. But it is very important that we do it."

I don't think I'm over-estimating the human race by making the observation that all of you would like to make the world a better place for having been here. Well—here's one way to do it! Invest your time. Because time, well invested, creates such a store of beautiful memories—moments in time that are yours forever. No one can take them away from you. When it is time for you to leave this world, the memories you helped to create stay behind long after you've gone. They live on in the hearts of those who knew and loved you. They are the stories people will tell about you—the things your children will pass along to your grandchildren.

Sooner or later there will come a time when you will be merely a memory. Your life and everything you were will be finally caught and held in a few precious and treasured remembrances. The wondrous potential of that legacy is in your hands right now—this very moment.

Why do elves work day in and day out in the North Pole Toy Shop? The answer is: we don't. The way we figure it, work is simply something you don't like to do. So we don't work; we give our time to what we love. Because of that, elves never manage to waste a second of their lives. Our time on this earth becomes an ongoing gift we exchange with each other. And in that joyous exercise, we reaffirm the glorious knowledge that life is a pleasure and living should be nothing less than a celebration of the gift of time.

So—get up off that sofa! Turn the television set off for a while. You'll get over the withdrawal. Don't put your love off—put it into action. Stop giving first-class attention to second-class clauses—er, causes. Go ahead! Live like there isn't going to be a tomorrow! Wish a stranger a Merry Christmas! Smile a little more. Have some fun again! Be healthier by being happier! All feelings, including happiness, depend on the brain's receiving and processing signals from the body. Your heart beats an additional three to five heartbeats a minute when you're happy. Happiness also improves blood circulation, causes your skin temperature to rise, and makes your muscles relax. That's a win-win no-brainer by anyone's standards!

Just remember along the way, in case you ever need it, the wonderful lesson old Ebenezer Scrooge learned:

> Some people laughed to see the alteration in him, but he let them laugh, and little heeded them; for he was wise enough to know that nothing ever happened on this globe for good, at which some people did not have their fill of laughter in the outset; and knowing that such as these would be blind anyway, he thought it quite as well that they should wrinkle up their eyes in grins, as have the malady in less attractive forms. His own heart laughed; and that was quite enough for him.

THE LOST CHILDREN

Grief fills the room up of my absent child ...
—WILLIAM SHAKESPEARE

The boss and his wife live in the Great Lodge at the North Pole. This place is every wonderful thing your imagination could possibly make it—and more. It sits at the center of the entire complex of lodges and buildings. Some people have always imagined that the toyshop is at the center of things, but it never was. It's neither the center geographically or ideologically. And I believe there's a fundamental lesson in this design.

The boss's family comes first—above anything. Everything he thinks, says, or does has family at the center of it. It's just the way he is. And I guess that makes us elves very lucky. We're part of his family. And we share in everything—the good times (which are frequent) and the not-so-good times (which are infrequent but inevitable—even for Santa Claus).

Now, you might imagine that the boss hits the floor every morning with Christmas on his mind. (In a way, he does, but

I'll explain that later.) You might think he can hardly wait to get to the Toy Shop each day. You might even imagine the amount of time he spends pouring over that infamous *Book of Names*—who's been naughty or nice—that sort of thing.

Nothing could be further from the truth.

Santa Claus begins a normal day very quietly. He takes his time in the morning—even when he is excited about getting to work. He uses this very special and private time to center himself—to take stock and plan the rest of the day in his mind. It doesn't take him very long at all—and the routine varies from time to time.

Sometimes he'll put some music on while he dresses. Sometimes he'll dress then sit quietly in his favorite chair for a few minutes, gazing silently out of the window. There are times he'll go for a quiet morning walk—all by himself.

I know for a fact that he talks to God during these morning private times. Some people might describe it as praying—and I guess you could say that. But, honestly, it's more like a private talk—a conversation. Sometimes God talks and Santa listens. Sometimes Santa talks and God listens. I know they both laugh together a great deal of the time.

(It's often been said that God has a terrific sense of humor. Most people just don't think of God in quite that light. Would anyone without a sense of humor have made an armadillo? Or a duck-billed platypus? Think about it.)

He places his family next on the list. When he's finished with his private morning time, he comes into the Dining Hall and joins everyone else. And because he's cared enough to take his private time each day, when he does enter the Dining Hall, he's already radiating with something extra special. (Most people will tell you that Santa Claus lights up a room when he enters. Well, this is why.)

Do you know what "working a room" means? Well, he's a master at it! His focus—his complete attention—is immediately on everyone else. And it's uncanny, but he always seems to know when someone needs an extra pat on the shoulder, a hug, a kind word, or even a gentle reprimand. (This may shock you, but elves aren't perfect either.)

Mrs. Claus is there with his usual mug of hot, spiced tea. He always gives her a kiss on the cheek when she hands it to him. (The tea is always served with a loving smile.) And let me tell you that this is routine—but not an empty routine. What they share—even the little times—is never taken for granted. They just don't do it unless they mean it. The beauty of their relationship is that, for the greater portion of the time, they *do* mean it. And it shows! It's that important to both of them—what you might call an investment.

By the way—did you know that the rest of the world didn't even realize there was a Mrs. Claus until a woman wrote about her for the first time in 1899? True. The writer's name was Katharine Lee Bates, and the title of her work was "Goody Santa Claus on a Sleigh-Ride." Catchy, huh? Still we were all genuinely happy for Mrs. Claus because it was time she began receiving the public acclaim she was rightfully due. (By the way, Katharine Lee Bates wrote thirty-two books. Most of them are long forgotten now. But don't feel too bad.

She managed to write one very lovely song—"America The Beautiful.")

They're a great team—the boss and his wife. They've taken the time—and the work it takes—to become secure with each other. They know, instinctively, what the other needs, and they're there to supply it.

Don't get me wrong. I don't think they always had it. In fact, I happen to know that it wasn't always smooth sailing, and they still don't always agree with each other. But I also know that the light in their bedroom doesn't go out until they do! Or at least until they honestly accept their agreement to have the freedom to sometimes disagree.

And they're very clear on the fact that disagreement doesn't mean rejection. (It only moves into that realm when you don't take the time to communicate.) And, brother, that's something they do on a daily basis. Someone once said that work is only something you don't want to do. But I happen to know that they honestly (but joyously) work at their relationship—and are wise enough to know it takes a little time every day. And sometimes I know it doesn't come easily for either one of them! Can you imagine what sort of pressure the boss and his wife constantly live with? We're talking Santa Claus here! I know you've heard the phrase about living in a fish bowl!

At five o'clock every day, the boss and his wife have their private time together. They go into the study and sit together on a large sofa in front of a great, stone fireplace—and visit. Sometimes they don't do anything but hold hands, letting the time pass in silence. I've even seen them share an occasional glass of sherry. But what makes those silences different from other times is the love contained at the center of it all. And because of this invested time together, they've always managed to keep a great deal of passion in their relationship. This is a pretty sizable accomplishment. Let's face it; they aren't spring chickens anymore. The courtship seems to keep going. It's kept them young. It's kept them strong. It's kept them together.

The boss and Mrs. Claus know that happiness is a decision. They mutually arrived at this long-term resolution ages ago. In retrospect, their decision was a very wise one and has kept them together for ages in joyous unison and quiet contentment.

There is a small, single room in a far wing of the Great Lodge that's officially off-limits to everyone but the boss himself. Of all the other rooms in the entire lodge, this one, given its location, is separated from the rest of the cheerful noise and bustle that always seems to fill the others.

It's a place he rarely visits. It wasn't until some careful, but distant, observation that we finally realized he would usually go off to this room just after some major, unpleasant world event had taken place. For many, many years, no one even knew what was in this room. It was Santa Claus's private place, and that was enough for us. We have great respect for the boss's desire for some occasional privacy and never once asked him about it. Of course we were curious. Elves are, by nature, very curious creatures. But since the boss never talked about the room to anyone, we always managed to keep our insatiable curiosity to ourselves. After all, when you're as much of a public figure as Santa Claus, you certainly deserve at least one quiet corner of the world where you can go to simply get away from things.

One day we had a sort of mini-emergency in the Toy Shop. It was nothing major—just a question of a deadline that had to be moved up. Still, all schedule changes have to be cleared by the boss himself. (If elves are curious creatures, we're also sticklers for proper procedure.) So, since I had the piece of paper in my hand at the time, I told the others that I would find the boss and get his okay on it.

The first place I looked was the study. He wasn't there. I couldn't find him in the Great Room or even the reindeer stables. For a moment or two I considered the fact that he might have gone out for one of his walks. But he never took a walk during this particular time of day, so I hesitated to bundle up and go out to look for him. I stood in the hallway, paper still in hand, trying to figure out where he might have gone.

Then it occurred to me to go to the closed door of that little faraway room and knock. That's where he was. It took a few moments before he answered, and when he did, his voice was soft and distant.

"Who is it?" he asked.

I cleared my throat and squared my shoulders. No one had ever intruded on his privacy in this room before. I was the first elf to do it, and I was very much aware of that fact.

"We've had a last-minute switch in a deadline," I said, speaking to the door. "We just need your okay on it." Then, almost as a second thought, I added, "I'll be happy to come back later if you'd like."

"No, no," I heard him reply softly, "I'll take a look at it now. Come in."

Well, you could've knocked me over with a feather! I had just been invited into a room no one had ever visited but the boss himself. This is something that happens very rarely—if at all—to anyone in the world. I had no idea what to expect. I hardly even knew how to react! Still, when the boss says come in, you do.

Slowly, and as quietly as possible, I turned the knob and eased the door open only wide enough to put my head in. The room was dark. There were several lights on, but the room was still a dark place. Have you ever noticed that different rooms in your own homes have different moods? A dining room has a mood that's quite different from, say, a playroom. This was very true here. It was as much the mood of the room that contributed to the feeling of darkness as it was the number of lights burning within it. And the mood of that room was undeniably dark.

The walls were mahogany—dark mahogany. There were several tables with lamps on them. But that was it! There was no other furniture in the entire room—nothing else except for a single, large easy chair right in the center of everything. Right in the middle of the room! It was made of leather— dark leather—and the whole chair swiveled on its base so it could face any direction. This was where the boss was sitting—when my eyes grew accustomed enough to locate him there.

"It's all right," he said softly, "Come on in." Still, he never looked at me directly. His gaze was somewhere else—some place distant—even beyond the walls of the room.

Instinctively I followed the direction of his gaze with my own eyes—just in case he happened to be in the room with someone else. And that's when I saw them! The pictures and photographs. There were hundreds of them. And they were everywhere!

It's difficult for me to describe it—the sheer amount of them. Lining the walls, sitting in antique frames on the two tables, some of them simply leaning against the walls along the perimeter of the room. Pictures and photographs of children! A few of them were so old that they were yellowed with age, and the edges of the paper were ragged and torn.

It was immediately obvious that the boss had taken great care to preserve all of them—but particularly the older ones. They had all been lovingly matted and framed behind glass. Some of the frames were priceless antique things with golden-gilt trim. Other frames were more modern in appearance. The older ones weren't photographs, but paintings or etchings. Some were nothing but black cutout silhouettes. Some were done with oil paint, some in watercolor. Some of the photographs were black and white and others were in full color. They were all sizes and shapes. But they were all pictures or photographs of children!

It was enough to take your breath away. And it did! I was unable to speak for a few minutes. To cover my awkward silence, I stepped into the room and quietly closed the door behind me. Once inside, I simply stood there, glancing around the room, looking into the faces of children who returned my gaze from picture frames numbering virtually in the hundreds.

Suddenly the boss sighed and shifted slightly in the great chair. He was bringing himself back from some place far beyond. Slowly he stretched out his hand toward me.

"Let's see the schedule change," he said.

His request snapped me back into reality. I walked briskly to his chair and handed him the slip of paper. He scanned it briefly and, after another moment of quiet consideration, nodded in agreement.

"We can do this," he nodded. I handed him a pen, and he scribbled his initials, SC, at the bottom of the paper then handed it back to me. I hesitated for a second more in case he had anything to add to the instructions. But he just sighed again and settled back in the great chair, returning his gaze to that place beyond the walls of the room.

Realizing that my official reason for staying there had passed, I turned and headed toward the door.

"Never expected anything like this, did you?" the boss asked just as I reached for the doorknob.

I froze! I didn't want him to think that I'd been prying. I had hoped he hadn't noticed my reaction to the pictures and photographs—even though he would've had to have been blind not to.

What do I say now? I asked myself in that brief moment of desperation. *What else?* came the silent answer from my heart. *The truth.*

I turned around to face him again. "I'm sorry," I stammered with some difficulty, "I didn't want to bother you."

The boss swiveled the great chair around so that he was facing me. And, for the first time in my life, I saw sadness in his eyes! Oh, I've seen him tired before. I've even seen him depressed and nervous. But I've never, ever seen him sad. And my heart came right up into my throat.

"Tell me what you see in this room," the boss said.

I swallowed hard, trying desperately to force my heart down and out of my voice.

"Hundreds of … children." I replied hoarsely.

"Pick one," he said.

"I don't understand what you mean," I answered.

"Pick a single face … a single pair of eyes," he explained quietly.

I took several steps toward the center of the room again and glanced around. I was still feeling awkward and hadn't yet recovered from the effect of finding so much sadness in the boss's eyes. So I just took a deep breath and pointed to one of the framed pictures. It wasn't that I would have necessarily picked that particular picture; it was just that I wanted to do something that would buy me a little more time to adjust.

From his place in that great chair, the boss studied the picture I had chosen. Finally he nodded slightly and, still gazing at the picture, he started to speak.

"That is the picture of a boy who lived in England in the sixteen hundreds. His mother and father were very poor. They worked every day from sunrise to sunset in order to simply survive. I think they truly loved the boy, but they never showed him any affection. I suppose they thought it was enough just to keep him alive. He wanted, very badly, to earn their love—some small, simple show of affection. A touch. A hug now and then.

"One day before the sun had even come up, that little boy took a small sack of seeds from his father's coat pocket and planted them in the family's little garden, located just behind their ramshackle house. He took the seeds without asking, of course, but he only did it because he thought he was helping his parents in some small way.

"When his father got up and discovered that the seeds had been taken and planted without his knowledge, he went into a rage. He beat that boy into unconsciousness and finally left him, broken and bleeding, on the back doorstep of the house. The boy was only seven years old. And that beating changed his life forever."

The boss paused in his story and cleared his throat. I could see tears in his eyes.

"Do you know who the comprachicos were?" he asked.

"No, I don't," I replied.

"In seventeenth-century Europe," he went on, "there were wandering bands of smugglers. They were called com-prachicos. Their stock in trade was buying children, deforming them, and then selling them to the aristocracy. The practice was permitted because the aristocracy thought it was fashionable to have freaks in court."

"Freaks?" I repeated out loud.

The boss nodded and sighed heavily.

"The comprachicos practiced certain … 'arts,'" he explained in slow, labored words. "These 'arts' included stunting children's growth, placing muzzles on their faces to deform them, slitting their eyes, dislocating their joints, and malforming their bones."

The boss lapsed into complete silence. The reason was obvious. Tears were streaming down his face, lining his white beard with the wet traces of his absolute sadness.

"And this little boy in the picture…" I began, fumbling for words, "…he was one of their victims?"

"In a way," the boss replied, "You could say he was a victim, but not of the comprachicos. You see, some years later he became the first comprachico. He's the one who actually began all of the horror that followed. It's all there, if you look closely enough at his picture on the wall—in his face and eyes. The hurt and pain of a seven-year-old boy. Pain that grew and malformed, like that bag of stolen seeds he planted to win his father's love."

The sheer force of the story staggered me backward several steps. I actually held out my hands to try to regain my balance. My head swirled with overlapping visions of deformed children. My ears filled immediately with the cries and screams of the victims of such terrible cruelty. It was a horrible moment—and one that I will remember for the rest of my life.

All of us, with ever-growing frequency, are routinely made aware of the terrors of this world. You can't check out of a supermarket without seeing the face of still another victim plastered across the pages of some tabloid newspaper. Freaks are still entertaining. People still fight and kill each other—and we are aware of it. There are still wars and famine and disease. And we are aware of it all. It is an inescapable reality—a reminder of how far the world has yet to go until all of humanity is able to stand, side by side, in the light of the sun.

But it's not until you are made to focus all the pain, hurt, and suffering into the shape of a single child—it's only then that it all takes a comprehensible form. We can be aware of the fact that six million Jews lost their lives in the death camps of a terrible war—men, women, and children. But we can't come close to comprehending any of it until we can look into the eyes of just one of the victims—eyes that stare mournfully back at you from a faded photograph world.

The boss's soft voice brought me back from the vivid ghosts of my own imaginings.

"I call this place The Room of Lost Children," he said, "My children. Children who might have grown up to bless the world—children who could have made such a wonderful difference."

The boss, with great effort, stood slowly in the center of the room. "Somewhere along the way, I lost these," he said, pointing toward the picture-covered walls, "or they lost me. They lost the spirit of what I represent."

"So I keep their pictures here—in this little room. And add to them. Once here, they never leave."

The boss moved slowly in one large circle, occasionally pointing out a single picture or photograph as he called out their names in a solemn roll call. Some of the names would have been familiar to anyone—Booth, Capone, Eichmann, Speck, Judas, Gacy, Manson. But these were not the faces of murderers. They were children—not the now-familiar adults seen on newsreels or in later photographs. The incredible thing to me was that so many of the faces were of smiling, happy children—faces that did not contain a single hint or glimmer of the terrible things that would eventually take the light of the world from each pair of eyes. Now I knew the real reason the room seemed so terribly dark! It wasn't that it was merely filled with darkness; it was haunted by it.

"Sometimes," the boss said, placing a hand on my shoulder, "I come here to remind myself of a few things. I mourn the loss of these children. But I also reaffirm, again and again, how important it is to save the ones who're still just on the brink. Maybe it would have made a more cheerful place to have displayed the pictures of the saved ones, but I just didn't think that was strong enough. I never want to stop trying as hard as I can try. As sad a reminder as this room is, it's what keeps me going."

We both paused to take a last gaze at those silent walls—walls that cried out in anguish and despair. Walls that echoed with a single, united plea from the souls of all lost children everywhere.

Then the boss flipped the light switch and everything was swallowed by even deeper darkness. We walked out of the room together and closed the door behind us. I've never been back. I don't need to. If I never knew why we do what we can to make this world a better place, I know now. And I'm going to make a difference.

It's taken a bit of time, but I've managed a great deal of study regarding human beings. One thing I've learned is that you like to refer to your species as "the human race." Not a stroll, mind you, or a walk. Not even an amble. The word you've chosen is "race." Well, pardon this elf for saying so, but that sounds as though life might be a bit hurried for you humans. And by its definition, a race generally consists of winners and losers. In which case, who are some of the losers in your human race?

A survey I read by your Institute of Medicine of the National Academy of Sciences estimates that up to 17 to 20 percent of all children have emotional problems—including depression, anxiety disorders, attention-deficit disorders, and psychosis. A much larger number suffer from what is known as adjustment disorders—responses to specific crises in their lives. If we don't begin the healing process in time, these problems are carried over into their adolescent years. The Carnegie Corporation recently completed a study on America's adolescents. The results surprised everyone but those of us closest to Santa Claus. We've known for a long time.

The study found that American adolescents spend an average of five minutes a day alone with their fathers and twenty minutes of such time with their mothers. On average, teenagers watch about twenty-one hours of television each week, compared to 5.6 hours spent on homework and only 1.8 hours reading for pleasure. The time that is spent with their families is generally devoted merely to meals or to watching television.

Another study tells us that nearly thirty percent of eighth-graders are home alone after school for two or more hours. Low-income students are most likely to be home alone for more than three hours. While adolescents devote most of their waking hours to the basics, such as school, homework, eating, chores, or paid employment, about 40 percent of their time—or five hours a day—is discretionary.

Finally, this same report sadly estimates that half of America's twenty million adolescents, ages ten to fifteen, are in danger of never reaching their full potential, in large part because of the opportunities they face for destructive activities in their free time. Their tendency toward violence is becoming alarming. Your National Education Association estimates that every day one hundred thousand students carry a gun into their classrooms; another study reports that 13 percent of all incidents involving guns in the schools are actually occurring in your elementary and preschools! Every single school day, six thousand, two hundred fifty of your teachers are threatened with injury, and two hundred sixty are actually assaulted. That's seventy-three thousand teachers assaulted per school year by their students!

These are your young people—most of them barely a few steps away from their childhoods—and you are being told that they are in danger. Not just in trouble, mind you—*danger*!

Who are your young people if not a living, breathing reflection of the values you have instilled in them? Who are your young people if not your greatest investment in the future of mankind? Who are your young people if not the truest, most personal motivation for the changes that must be made in this world? Who are your young people that you should deny them the right to grow strong and keen in mind and body? Who are your young people that you should withhold from them the greatest single gift you could possibly ever give—your time and interest?

Right now, I don't believe they feel they even have your undivided attention.

I saw the consequences of the apathy of past generations mirrored in the eyes of the children peering at me from the pictures and photographs in that solitary room of the Great Lodge. That is why I know what I have to do. If only one photograph is kept from the walls in the Room of Lost Children because of something I said or did, my life will have mattered. And one more child will be able to keep forever the light of hope in his eyes!

CHRISTMAS MOURNING

Backward, turn backward, O Time, in your flight.
Make me a child again just for tonight.

—ELIZABETH AKERS ALLEN

That's right—*mourning*. It's a very, very real part of the holiday season. Not many people realize that, but it's very true. Sure, you've all heard of the post-Christmas syndrome. It's how the professionals refer to that psychological letdown that starts to hit you on Christmas day afternoon. It usually sets in about the time you take a moment's pause to gaze at the mountains of shredded wrapping paper, crumpled boxes, and ribbon scattered around your living room. It's that little, gnawing feeling that creeps into your soul when you amble into the kitchen for a late Christmas day snack—only to find there's not a clean glass or dish in the entire house. It's "peas on earth." Turkey bones and untouched cranberries are everywhere! Pots, pans, and dishes, stacked to the ceiling, blot out the light! On top of that, the Christmas tree is shedding needles like crazy—drying up before your unbelieving gaze! Depressing.

You don't really want to watch TV either, because they're just going to be running *It's a Wonderful Life*. A tearjerker if Frank Capra ever made one! And who in their right mind needs to spend a single minute of their Christmas holiday crying? And the answer is—almost every biggle in the world!

This is probably one of the unique secrets about Christmas. It's secret because hardly anyone admits to feeling less than wonderful during the Christmas holidays—except for what's normally allowed. Being tired and rushed is always allowed. Everyone can complain about that (and does)—so long, of course, as it's that sort of good-natured exasperation that everybody else seems to be going through too. Sharing complaints of that nature is expected—and relatively harmless in the long run. Besides, procrastination is a very human trait. Given a choice, most people put off things until they absolutely have to do them—like Christmas shopping. If that weren't a fact of life, shopping malls would be veritable ghost towns on Christmas Eve, and everyone would be home, savoring the simple joys of one of the most special evenings of the year!

Now, to really understand what happens to a biggle during the holidays, you have to accept, first of all, an axiom. It is simply this: all things are created twice. This simply means that your impressions of Christmas have two dimensions; the first dimension is the actual occurrence. It might be one particular Christmas family gathering or a certain toy you received while you were a little. The second dimension becomes your memory of the actual occurrence—how you remember that particular family gathering or that favorite toy.

So the actual event is the first dimension, and your memory of that event becomes the second dimension—and, in many ways, the most lasting and important. Because what actually happened on a particular Christmas past doesn't matter half as much as how you *remember* it!

Human memory is such an amazing thing! (An elf's memory works almost exactly the same, only sharper.) You can take a moment from life and keep it forever in your heart. It comes back to you the second you recall it—sometimes even when you don't consciously choose to do so. Memories roll back into your conscious thoughts like waves from the great ocean of experience. And, like waves, that motion is continuous and rhythmic. Your memories also bring back a great many emotional connections that affect the way you live in and deal with the present.

Once, I ate some shrimp that had gone bad. (We don't get a lot of shrimp at the North Pole, so they're really a delicacy to elves.) The bad shrimp made me ill. For years afterward, all I had to do was smell a bowl of steamed shrimp, and I began to feel nauseated! The memory actually affected me physically. And as much as I had always enjoyed shrimp, all I could do after that single, bad experience was sit in the Great Lodge, watching all the other elves happily pig out on what would have been my share of shrimp!

One bowl of bad shrimp—one vivid memory recalled—and it made me physically ill! That's how powerful memory can be. It's true of elves as well as people. Your human brain is like a gigantic butterfly net. And particular moments are the beautiful, sometimes illusive, butterflies. By the time you become a biggle, you've managed to amass quite a collection!

If one bowl of bad shrimp can make an elf physically ill years after the actual moment, imagine what a memory of a particular Christmas can do! It can affect the way you react to each succeeding Christmas for years to come. If your memories are warm and wonderful, it stands to reason that your succeeding Christmas holidays will have a better chance of being so too. If, for reasons, you sustain a Christmas hurt or disappointment, then the way your soul and body react to an approaching holiday is directly related to the memory of that experience. Memories can become like tinted lenses through which we view the entire scope of the present.

But here's something else to consider—even about those warm and wonderful memories. Generally, whenever biggles think about Christmas, they tend to think about Christmases past. In doing so, they often include memories of loved ones with whom they shared those past Christmases. Often, and sadly, those loved ones we choose to remember—grandmothers, grandfathers, mothers, fathers—are no longer in the world. So even warm and wonderful memories of Christmases past can be (and usually are) tinged with a bittersweet quality—something we often find hard to define or even understand. But a certain degree of sadness is as much a part of Christmas as mistletoe and firelight! Missing loved ones who are no longer with us is a natural and inevitable part of all of our holiday celebrations—but particularly at Christmas time.

Biggles also tend to miss their youth during this time of year. As I explained earlier, Christmas is a time when that little inside us would like very much to come out and play. That little in us all is only a breath away from our consciousness during Christmas. The wonderful smells of a fresh fir tree, cinnamon tea brewing on a stove, peppermint candy, or a turkey roasting in the oven of a warm cheery kitchen can, like the *Starship Enterprise* hitting warp overdrive, hurl you back to the days of your youth with the dizzying speed of light. In your mind's eye, you are suddenly standing in the kitchen you remember when you were young. You can see—actually *see*—your mother as you choose to remember her when she too was younger, preparing the Christmas turkey or those wonderful holiday cookies. And the exquisite pain of that single, incredible moment—the instant that wave of memory crashes to shore with such amazing emotional force—can literally take your breath away!

Have you ever seen biggles do that? Ever seen them walk into a kitchen during Christmas time and stop dead in their tracks? Have you ever seen a hand move involuntarily to their chests or to their mouths? You are witnessing a "memory wave" hitting the iceberg of consciousness. The little has just come to the surface of its being. And all it has to do is make that split decision to either let the little out or force everything back down inside.

By the time you become a biggle, you've collected a good many memories. Believe it or not, that actually happens to be one of the perks of becoming older. You see, people aged twenty to twenty-four are sad for an average of 3.4 days per month as opposed to just 2.3 days for people aged sixty-five to seventy-four. If you ask me, the happiness factor has to do with being able to pull up a happy memory when it's most needed.

Just because biggles sometimes make the decision to force everything back down inside doesn't mean they don't earnestly wish to connect with that little—or with the true meaning of Christmas, for that matter. It's just that surrendering to the emotional release of that experience has become something foreign to them—something to be avoided because they fear a loss of control. Biggles like to feel they are in control. They want to feel in control of their lives, their "things," their destinies, their emotions, their world—everything! Perhaps it's because when they were littles, they got the impression that this is what biggles do. After all, littles are controlled by biggles almost all of the time. So it's only natural that they relate biggle-ness to an ability to always be in control.

On the other hand, perhaps biggles want so much to be in control because, as they grow older, they begin to realize how little control they actually do have—or ever have had! And they panic. (I'm only an elf, so I can't really say for sure. These are merely observations, you understand.)

Humans, by nature, do like to share things. Most of all, they love to share laughter! There's nothing so wonderful as seeing several thousand people laughing together. A circus, a comedy in a theatre, it doesn't matter where or what. People will sit next to total strangers and share the gift of laughter with them! Absolutely marvelous! Public speakers always try to relax their audiences by telling a joke. Our greatest role models have been the ones who taught us that it's okay to laugh at ourselves. Romantic imaginings have always created heroes who laughed in the face of danger. (In real life, that trait usually demonstrates a severe lack of common sense.) The bottom line here is that laughter is a common bond that binds us all together on this planet.

So is sadness. If we are bound by laughter, we are equally bound by our tears. But tears are not what people prefer to share with each other, given the choice—and that's understandable. I'm certainly not recommending that everyone walk around sobbing on each other's shoulder all the time. Maybe just some of the time.

When we channel it properly, emotional release is quite healing. After all, crying is one of the first ways humans learn to communicate with the world! A hungry baby can't tell you it's hungry. The baby cries. (If nothing else, someone crying will certainly get your attention.) Crying is a fundamental mode of expression and emotional release. Tears, like laughter, can be some of the best medicine we ever take.

So—what do crying, bad shrimp, laughter, memories, and childhood have to do with Christmas mourning? Sometimes more than we realize. As much as we look forward to the holiday season, as much as we joyfully anticipate the togetherness of family and friends, as much as we need the experience of laughter shared, as much as all of this, we also need to go through a bit of healthy Christmas mourning.

What is Christmas really all about? Be careful not to repeat a memorized answer or go for the conditioned knee-jerk response here. It's time for you to give the question some very serious thought. Because as long as you allow someone else to define it for you, the chances of you ever knowing the joys of personal fulfillment remain slim. It's like the story of the man who searched for happiness all his life—and never found it. On his deathbed, someone asked him what happiness was. The man thought about it for a moment, smiled, sighed, and died. In that split second, he'd realized it after all. For him, perhaps happiness was simply defining the source of his search—something he had never stopped to do. We've got a generation of people out there searching for something—and most of them don't even know what that something really is.

Christmas became a national holiday in America on June, 26, 1870. You've been celebrating it ever since. So—we're back to the original question: What is Christmas really all about?

Okay. Here goes:

Christmas is about meeting needs.

Works for me. How about you? Spiritual needs, emotional needs, physical needs, religious needs, mental needs—

you name it. There are some things in life that all human beings need and require. There are some things in life that only certain individuals need—or perhaps we all need the same thing only in different quantities. This need we all harbor is obviously with us all year long—but it is most particularly felt during the holiday season. This is because, aside from everything else, all of us need some bit of magic in our lives. And of all other times during the entire year, Christmas provides us with the opportunity.

Let me quickly identify what I mean when I refer to a magical Christmas. And I can best do that by simply pointing out one of the things I don't mean. I don't mean Christmas is magical in the sense that we just go to bed on Christmas Eve and everything gets done for us. That isn't magic; it's laziness. And just in case any of you believe that the story of the shoemaker and the elves is an exception to the rule, go back and re-read it. The old shoemaker and his wife did their fair share of work in the scheme of things. Happiness isn't just handed to you on a silver platter—not even in a fairy tale. Santa Claus is nearer than anyone realizes—but you do have to go and meet him. You also have to go and meet your own needs in other aspects of your life on this planet. And remember that it can't truly be called a voyage until you've lost sight of the shore.

There is a lot of tradition connected to the celebration of this very special holiday. And family is a great part of it all. When we used to think of an "average" family, we knew that meant a father, a mother, and two children. These were the same families that went "over the river and through the woods" to Grandmother's house for the holidays. This memory of the past is the strongest emotional connection many people have to Christmas. And a great deal of human mourning is taking place because of changes in the world's traditional concept of family structure.

Today one in four American children grow up in a single-parent family. Census numbers from 1990 show that more than three million grandparents are raising their children's children.

Parents now regularly separate, divorce, and remarry—sometimes more than once. The "traditional" family has been transformed into the "contemporary" family—and we all need to be a bit more aware of that fact.

Everyone prepares for Christmas. And this preparation has, over a period of time, taken on the trappings of ceremony. Ceremony is a very important part of human existence—but, by no means, is it the heart or center of it at all. Technique is important to art in the same respect—so important, in fact, that technique is often mistaken for art. So the ceremony of Christmas is often mistaken for Christmas itself. For that matter, the ceremony of living is often mistaken for life. The truth is that a contemporary society is always going to have a few difficulties with its traditional ceremonies. That is why a certain amount of spiritual preparation (alignment) is also an ongoing need.

Some of this Christmas preparation is a conscious effort on your part. You make a conscious effort to drag the same decorations down from the attic year after year. You make a conscious effort to go out and buy a tree. You make a conscious effort to say to yourself: "This year, I'm going to get it all done on time for once in my life." You are aware of your actions and make conscious efforts on behalf of your own personal preparation for this special time of year. But it is important to understand that some of your preparation is also subconscious. You do it without thinking about it at all. You hear Christmas music, and immediately something happens. You experience a conditioned knee-jerk reaction while your automatic pilot light flickers on. You place the same ornaments on the same kind of tree each year. The same Christmas decorations go in their traditional places throughout your home. If you've always gone to midnight mass, you'll make every effort to continue that habit. You may even have traditional gifts that are on your shopping list each and every year for the same people. (Who said Dad should always get a necktie?) You approach the entire holiday season by slipping into a carefully controlled and manipulated glide path that you hope will ultimately land you under the tree on Christmas morning. Is there any wonder that so many are so often … disappointed?

Time sets a great example. It moves forward—and so should we. The past is a great place to visit—but you wouldn't really want to live there. It's just that, especially during the holidays, people tend to cling to some great expectation of having to redo things as they have always been done. Or perhaps at least they try to finally get it right for once. This can lead to more than a little frustration and anxiety when what you think is supposed to happen doesn't happen. That's because you've confused the celebration of Christmas with the reincarnation of the past. Right away you've set tremendous limitations on the amount of joy you will ever be able to experience. Recycled joy may be better than no joy at all... but not by much.

Since Christmas is also a time for family, it also stands to reason that Christmas is a time for trying to meet their needs as well as yours. Now, there you are—trying to come to terms with what your own personal needs are, and the house is filling up with noisy relatives. Or is it? Perhaps some thought ought to be given to what it now means to be part of a contemporary family. You also need to understand that the term *contemporary* doesn't mean that families are, out of modern necessity, "nontraditional." This isn't the case at all. But we do live in the moment. We live and breathe in the now. We are all, therefore, contemporary. And, in the truest sense, we all also belong to one family. I don't think I could tell you how many elves live and work at the North Pole. I've lost count. What I can tell you is that each and every elf who lives at the North Pole is part of one gigantic, loving and extended family. So perhaps it's time for all of us to try to be a little more sensitive to the makeup and needs of the families to which we belong. It's also important for you to understand that you have *Yesterday* families as well as *Today* families. And while you should always remember and cherish what your Yesterday family was, you also need to see it as what it has become.

Not myth. Not memory. Not something created in a lovely Frank Capra film. We need to see it—*really* see it—as it is.

You need to understand that when you mourn the past, you are sometimes merely mourning the time you've lost to your own spiritual adolescence. There is nothing intrinsically wrong with this—so long as you understand that you have also, hopefully, moved beyond what you once were. You've been around long enough to have identified a few of your needs. You've also learned that part of living is having to eventually get about the business of meeting the needs you've identified.

You humans have all sorts of cognitive biases that make it easy to forget the good things, or you simply let the bad things overshadow them. The truth is that you actually have to work to keep them from disappearing from your memory altogether. One of the quickest, easiest ways to do that is to set a specific time to remember. How hard could that be? Turn off the television set, gather the family around the hearth, and share memories of Christmas! It might well be the most meaningful holiday gift you've ever given or received. The gift, of course, is always to the giver.

The ancient Romans gave themselves a holiday that served as a sort of catalyst for all of this. It was called Juvenalia, the festival of childhood and youth. It was a time for celebrating what you once were as a way of finding deeper meaning and contentment with what you had become. This holiday was always begun on the first day of January. What a splendid way to start a new year!

I'll tell you something I've noticed about you humans. It has to do with one particular, private little Christmas Eve ceremony many of you allow yourselves. Know what it is? I'm amazed at the number of you who steal yourself a bit of private time and find a reason to go outside on Christmas Eve. Some of you simply step out on the doorstep in order to take a deep breath of night air. Some of you take a walk around the block. Some go to church—or to visit friends. The thing is, you all seem to find your own personal reasons for going outside.

There's something so incredibly special about that one night. It's in the air—almost tangible, something profoundly beautiful and calming to the soul. Christmas Eve has had that effect on many people over the years. In 1865, for example, an Episcopal rector named Phillips Brooks was traveling through the Holy Land. He had arranged his schedule so that he would be in Bethlehem on Christmas Eve. When evening fell at the end of that very special day, he rode on horseback to a hill overlooking the town. There he spent most of the night gazing down on the sacred beauty before him. Then, almost without thinking, he pulled paper and pencil from his coat pocket. Wanting, somehow, to capture what he was seeing and feeling, he began to jot down a few lines of poetry.

Three years later, the young clergyman gave the five verses of his poem to Lewis Redner, his organist and Sunday school superintendent. Brooks asked his friend if he might consider setting the poem to music. Redner shook his head in quiet desperation. It was December once again, and his obligations as organist at the Church of the Advent and Holy Trinity in Philadelphia were considerable. He didn't know how he'd possibly find the time—or inspiration—at least not with everything else there was to do. Still, he told Brooks he would try.

For a week Redner struggled with the task. But nothing seemed to satisfy him. Nothing seemed to do the poetry justice. Something was missing, and Redner knew it. He finally went to bed on Christmas Eve—still disappointed in himself for not being able to think of a melody, a few satisfactory notes.

Later that night, he awoke from a deep sleep and turned to gaze out of his window at the beautiful star-filled sky—a sky very much like the sky his friend had seen over Bethlehem. In that moment, the music came to him! It literally poured from his heart and soul onto the manuscript paper—finished and complete. In the years to come, Redner would always refer to the tune as his very own "gift from heaven." It was a bequest he and Phillip Brooks shared with the rest of the world—a gift that continues to bring that same world closer together. Today we still know the poetry and music as an endearing Christmas song entitled "O Little Town of Bethlehem." And how about the most famous Christmas carol of all—"Silent Night." It wasn't just written about Christmas Eve—it was written *on* a Christmas Eve. It was written in the Austrian village of Oberndorf on Christmas Eve, 1818. But that's another story.

The truth is that we all find our own Juvenalias eventually. And there is always something bittersweet in each of them. One important Juvenalia in all of our lives is the permission we give ourselves to grieve. You do need to occasionally remind yourself that it's okay to miss loved ones, to miss your youth, to miss what was, to miss all those things that make humans human. It is allowed. You need to know that it's perfectly all right to hear Christmas music and be moved to tears. It's alright to watch your littles performing in a school's Christmas pageant and be moved to tears. It's all right to be together with old friends during the holidays and be moved to tears. It's all right to walk into a kitchen, inhale those wonderful smells, and be moved to tears. It's all right to meet your own needs where all of this is concerned. It is allowed. Christmas mourning has as much a place in your celebration as any other emotion you're going to experience during the entire holiday season. In fact, a little healthy Christmas mourning will actually enable you to add more depth to the rest of your feelings. All you're doing is simply blowing a little carbon out of the pipes. You're cleaning out your emotional insides in preparation for being able to truly celebrate the holiday season. You're making more room for joy! And that's not a bad recipe for Christmas at all.

And once you've gone there—grieved a little, given vent to some honest mourning, taken care of a little spiritual housecleaning—you can better separate yourself from the inevitable holiday depression and sadness. Just remember—

take the *u* out of the word *mourning*, and what you have is a new day!

That's when you finally begin to understand what a Merry Christmas is really all about!

THE REALNESS OF SANTA CLAUS

The little world of childhood with its familiar surroundings
is a model of the greater world. The more intensively
the family has stamped its character upon the child,
the more it will tend to feel and see its earlier miniature
world again in the bigger world of adult life.

—CARL GUSTAV JUNG

Everyone believes in something—even if it's only the assumption that there's nothing at all left to believe in. But even that's still belief in something! And it's better than nothing—though not by very much. In other words, there's always something to believe in. It's merely a question of choice.

A little girl named Virginia O'Hanlon once wrote Francis P. Church a letter in which she stated that her friends were telling her there was no such thing as Santa Claus. She wanted to know if that was true or not. After giving it a bit of thought, Church decided to set the record straight. His reply to Virginia was also a priceless gift to the rest of the world ... a wonderful defense regarding the realness of Santa Claus that has since become history's most reprinted newspaper editorial. It is, in fact, such a brilliant defense, it deserves to be reprinted here. If it's been a while since you've read it in its entirety, it'll certainly be worth the time it may take to refresh your memory.

Virginia, your little friends are wrong. They have been affected by the skepticism of a skeptical age. They do not believe except [what] they see. They think that nothing can be which is not comprehensible by their little minds. All minds, Virginia, whether they be men's or children's, are little. In this great universe of ours man is a mere insect, an ant, in his intellect, as compared with the boundless world about him, as measured by the intelligence capable of grasping the whole of truth and knowledge.

Yes, Virginia, there is a Santa Claus. He exists as certainly as love and generosity and devotion exist, and you know that they abound and give to your life its highest beauty and joy. Alas! How dreary would be the world if there were no Santa Claus. It would be as dreary as if there were no Virginias. There would be no childlike faith then, no poetry, no romance to make tolerable this existence. We should have no enjoyment, except in sense and sight. The eternal light with which childhood fills the world would be extinguished.

Not believe in Santa Claus! You might as well not believe in fairies! You might get your papa to hire men to watch in all the chimneys on Christmas Eve to catch Santa Claus, but even if they did not see Santa Claus coming down, what would that prove? Nobody sees Santa Claus, but that is no sign that there is no Santa Claus. The most real things in the world are those that neither children nor men can see. Did you ever see fairies dancing on the lawn? Of course not, but that's no proof that they are not there. Nobody can conceive or imagine all the wonders there are unseen and unseeable in the world.

You may tear apart the baby's rattle and see what makes the noise inside, but there is a veil covering the unseen world which not the strongest man, nor even the united strength of all the strongest men that ever lived, could tear apart. Only faith, fancy, poetry, love, romance, can push aside that curtain and view and picture the supernal beauty and glory beyond. Is it all real? Ah, Virginia, in all this world there is nothing else real and abiding.

No Santa Claus! Thank God! He lives, and he lives forever. A thousand years from now, Virginia, nay, ten times ten thousand years from now, he will continue to make glad the heart of childhood.

During all the time I've worked for and been associated with the boss, I've never once heard him try to convince a single soul that he's real. And, take it from one who knows, he's been in belief situations that would try the patience of a saint! If he had a quarter for every time some little, perched on his lap in a department store, asked him if he was real, he'd be a very wealthy person today!

It's always puzzled me too why any little—perched on Santa's knee and running sticky, candy-coated fingers through his beard—would stop to wonder if it were a real person's knee and a real person's beard.

Littles must be very confused about reality sometimes! But, then, they do live in a very confused and confusing world. Biggles have a hard enough time trying to make sense of things, constantly wandering around, asking themselves, "Is this really the way I feel?" or "Is this honestly what I want?" In other words, they spend a great deal of time second guessing what's real and what's merely an impression of reality. Add to that the preconceived notion, hammered into their consciousness since birth, that they should be doing what everybody else is doing, and you can see why adult stress levels are at all time highs. No wonder littles pick up the doubting habit so early in life! No wonder they need a little occasional reassurance while sitting on Santa's knee.

In a very beautiful play by Luigi Pirandello, one of his characters says, "I only know that when I was a child, I thought the moon in the pond was real. How many things I thought real. I believed everything I was told and I was happy!"

When you go to a movie or a play, you're requested to suspend your disbelief—at least to a degree. Suspending disbelief for a few hours is the way you commit to the special magic of any theatrical production. You know, for instance, that the character of Don Quixote in *Man of La Mancha* is being played by an actor. You know he doesn't actually die during the last act of the show while singing "The Impossible Dream." But, if you're able to suspend enough of your disbelief, you will sit there in your seat and weep at it all! (Some theatergoers can suspend enough disbelief to enjoy a veritable emotional smorgasbord!)

The practice of suspending your disbelief is a nice habit whether you attend the theatre or not. Entrepreneurs do it all the time! Remember, there was a time when people believed no one could fly. The thought that man could fly was an illusion. The Wright brothers simply suspended their disbelief in what appeared to be an illusion. The next thing they suspended was a motor-driven airplane—in mid-air! So you see what can happen when you start committing to the possibilities.

We spend a large portion of our lives developing beliefs. These beliefs are grounded in experience and, more often than not, serve us well. But occasionally we can take one or two of those beliefs and, while focusing on them alone, try suspending our associated disbelief.

Do you think it was easy for the first flying reindeer to take that initial death-defying leap of faith? Au, contraire! Let me assure you that for the first five hundred feet of the free-fall there was an incredible amount of deer screaming, followed—of course—by a growing sense of self-assurance coupled with a brazen display of mind-blowing aerial acrobatics. The point here is that whenever we're brave enough to put our beliefs to a test, whole new horizons begin to open up. We tend to begin to look at things as being possible instead of always impossible. At the very least, chances are better that we won't disregard the possibility of something else just because it doesn't seem to exist within the realm of the currently accepted belief.

The comfortable thing about this approach to life is that it's positive. It's also a sure guarantee that, as long as we can accept possibilities, we'll also never cease to explore, learn, and grow.

This brings us back to the topic at hand—the realness of Santa Claus. It's a belief that most people are going to examine at some point in their lives. In fact, it's one of the very first belief struggles you'll probably get into—a special struggle because it's something that's often done in private.

It generally begins when a little hears someone say, "There's no such thing as Santa Claus." The little who hears this for the first time usually has a very logical response: "Are you crazy? I've sat on his knee and pulled his beard!"

"Oh, sure," the argument then goes, "but that wasn't the real Santa Claus."

Following that sort of logic, a lot of people's hair isn't real either. Why? Because a lot of people have hair that is no longer its natural color. So, because the color isn't natural, the aforementioned logic would have us believe that the hair isn't real either. Well, folks, if color-treated hair isn't real hair, we've got an awful lot of bald-headed people walking the streets. And somebody better get them this vital information in a hurry!

Okay, now for a little ORC (obvious religious connotation). I said we'd stay away from it as long as possible—and I've kept my word. But there's just no way around the obvious point that no one has seen God either.

Even Moses had to talk to a burning bush! Can you blame the Children of Israel for going a little berserk when he came down from the mountain, carrying the Ten Commandments? With all due respect to Charlton Heston, I don't believe Moses really made such a grand entrance into the midst of the Hebrew children—who, by the way, had decided to party down with a golden idol in his absence.

"Hold on!" Moses says, "What you're doing is all wrong."

"Oh yeah?" comes the reply, "Says who?"

"God says so!" Moses informs them.

"Yeah?" continues the retort, "You saw God up on that mountain?"

"As a matter of fact," Moses concludes, "I did."

Now, Moses had to be grimacing when he said that because he knew the obvious comeback was going to finally get around to "What did God look like?"

Can you imagine the expressions on their faces when Moses told them God was a burning bush? They probably stood around in absolute silence for a few minutes, just waiting for the punch line! Here is this man, standing at the foot of a mountain with ten rules carved in stone tablets—ten rules the entire world should live by, rules he got straight from a burning bush! And some people have a hard time trying to understand why the Children of Israel may have thought Moses was just a bubble or two off plumb.

The obvious point here is that just because God appeared in the form of a burning bush doesn't mean God is a bush. The spirit of Christmas may choose to appear in the form of Santa Claus. That doesn't mean that the spirit of Christmas is Santa Claus. But the spirit of Christmas can take the form of Santa Claus—just like God can take the form of a burning bush.

Look at it from another point of view. Can you sit on the knee of a spirit and tell it what you want for Christmas? In a very real way you can. You have! Seen any burning bushes lately? I don't know. But have you ever noticed how a Christmas tree can appear to blaze with light? Might a Christmas tree even be considered a burning bush of sorts? Up to you. But remember that your job is to try to consider the possibilities!

And, speaking of trees, light, and possibilities, decorating Christmas trees began in Germany as far back as the tenth century. It's generally believed that Martin Luther was the one who started it all. The story goes that he was out walking one beautiful Christmas Eve. The night sky was wondrously clear and lit by millions of twinkling stars. The sight so moved Martin Luther that he uprooted a small fir tree and took it back home with him. There he fixed little wax candles to the branches of the tree and lit them. This was done to remind children of the beautiful heavens from which Christ descended to save the world. By 1604, the idea had taken hold, and decorating fir trees was a fairly common practice.

According to Charles Greville, a nineteenth-century diarist, the first Christmas tree in England was put up by a German, Princess Lieven. Most Englishmen will tell you that Prince Albert was the one who introduced the Christmas tree to England. But he was actually ten years behind Princess Lieven. What Prince Albert did do—along with Queen Victoria, of course—was popularize the custom of having the Christmas tree become the central feature of the family Christmas. Victoria wrote that the custom of decorating a fir tree, together with sounding trumpets to herald in the New Year, "quite affected dear Albert who turned pale, and had tears in his eyes, and pressed my hand very warmly." In 1841, she also noted: "Today I have two children of my own to give presents to, who, they know not why, are full of happy wonder at the German Christmas tree and its radiant candles."

Do you know who had the very first Christmas tree decorated with electric lights? Thomas Edison. Who else! In 1882, only three years after he had given the world his invention of the light bulb, Edison's coworkers hand-blew tiny bulbs and wired them to a tree as a surprise for him. Still, it wasn't until 1903 that the idea really caught on and the very first strings of electric Christmas tree lights were sold by General Electric. Before that, John Barth, a German Methodist minister in Louisville, Kentucky, had come up with the idea of decorating Christmas trees with tiny oil lamps. Instead of the exposed flame of a candle, the flames produced by Barth's tiny oil lamps were protected by little glass globes. Barth got his patent in 1887.

After the custom of decorating Christmas trees caught on, what had to happen next? Two Philadelphians, Hermann Albrecht and Abram C. Mott, received the first US patents for Christmas tree stands! That was in 1876. The first electric revolving tree stand was patented by Alfred Wagner of St. Louis in 1899.

The oldest known reference to Christmas trees in America comes from the same people who passed out the first Christmas presents in the New World—the Moravians. On Christmas Day, 1747, in Bethlehem, Pennsylvania, there were "several small pyramids and one large pyramid of green brushwood...all decorated with candles and the large one with apples and pretty verses."

Incredible, isn't it? What started out as a gentle and beautiful reminder to the children of the world didn't waste any time in becoming an incredibly large and mechanized industry. Christmas tree lots spring up like mushrooms before the Thanksgiving dishes have even been washed and put away! Most people don't know where the custom of decorating trees came from—or why. To be honest, most people don't really care. All most people know is they had better rush out and buy one of the darned things while the pickings are good. There are so many things about the celebration of Christmas that were put in place to be reminders to us. The sad thing about it all is that we've somehow forgotten what it was we were supposed to remember. We have Christmas trees, mistletoe, wassail toasts, and Yule logs. We just don't know what they symbolize—or used to symbolize—and why that symbolism is even important anymore. The same thing is becoming true about the symbol of Santa Claus.

A lot of people say the legend surrounding Santa Claus first began with a man known as St. Nicholas. Other than that, there isn't very much more we know about this man— except that he was born in Lycia (now part of Turkey), lived there all his life, became its Archbishop, and died there sometime in the first part of the fourth century AD. What we do know about St. Nicholas is that he became one of the most popular saints of the Middle Ages. In fact, he was so popular that he was adopted as patron saint by pawnbrokers, brewers, pilgrims, parish clerks, coopers, travelers, boatmen, Aberdeen, Russia, and those who had unjustly lost lawsuits!

But we primarily remember him as being the patron saint of children. St. Nicholas's Feast Day was traditionally celebrated on December sixth, when children were presented gifts of gingerbread or toys. Are you beginning to see how it's all evolved through the years?

To make things easier to grasp, you've got to understand one thing: Santa Claus has a lot of helpers—thousands upon thousands of them. Some of them only chip in around Christmas time. Others work at it all year long. Some are very good at what they do. Others—well...at least they give it a shot and hang on to their day jobs.

Since there are thousands upon thousands of helpers and only one real Santa Claus, chances are that you're going to run into a helper more often than you're going to bump into the real McCoy. It's just the law of averages.

Put another way: the world is also full of bushes. God chose only one of them to appear in for Moses. It's the same principle with Santa's helpers. Every now and then one of them gets chosen. The thing is you never know which one. And don't always think you're going to better your chances by looking only in the nicest, most expensive places. Here again it's well to remember that God didn't choose a giant redwood. Just a little bush.

Consider a few more points. Was God any less real for choosing to appear as a burning bush? Is the spirit of Christmas any less real for choosing to sometimes appear as a jolly old fat man in a red suit? It's true that a few people might get the impression that God is only a burning bush—just like some people believe that the spirit of Christmas is only Santa Claus. This happens because people are limited only by their imaginations. And some people's imaginations are only ... limited.

We tend to refer to these kinds of people as being extremely literal. They can deal wonderfully with spreadsheets, but have a very tough time with original ideas. They live in a tangible realm of literal existence. If they can't touch it, taste it, smell it, or hear it—and preferably all at the same time—then it just isn't real to them. Well, Santa Claus is, more often than not, a very tangible presence around Christmas time. If you're heavy into the literal realm of existence, then Santa's just about *it* as far as December 25th is concerned.

You've probably heard about London's Big Ben. It's a clock, right? One of the most famous clocks in the whole world? Right? Wrong. Big Ben is not a clock. It is a bell—located in the clock tower of the Houses of Parliament. It's been there since 1859—long enough for people to become a bit confused.

For years, every time Big Ben chimed, people looked toward the direction of the sound. What did they see? A clock. So, naturally, they began to associate the name of the bell they heard to the sight they saw. Never mind that Big Ben is a bell—a thirteen-ton bell, at that—nine feet in diameter and seven and a half feet tall. As far as most people are concerned, it's a clock. The perception has become the reality—a reality that happens to be based on an incorrect assumption.

So if you look at Christmas and all you see is Santa Claus (or one of his helpers), you're seeing only part of the picture. You're seeing what the spirit of Christmas has become for some people. In other words, you're looking at a bell and calling it a clock. And if the Santa Claus you're looking at doesn't happen to fulfill all your expectations, it's easy to say he isn't real. And maybe that particular Santa Claus isn't. I mean, I know one rotten apple can spoil a whole barrel, but to say Santa Claus doesn't exist—*period*—is a rather sweeping statement to make based on one minor disappointment. The truth is that it really doesn't matter if you don't believe in Santa Claus. The most important thing to know is that he believes in you.

Unfortunately, there are some people who've managed to convince themselves that they don't need Santa Claus to be real. (Don't ask me why; just accept the fact.) And for those people—the unbelievers—Santa Claus doesn't exist. These are the same people who'll hear Big Ben chiming away, glance up at the clock, and then say, "I didn't hear that. Did you?" But it's their reality—and they're certainly permitted to have one.

A few people once became so concerned about how Santa Claus was being perceived that a group of them even formed The Santa Claus Association in New York during 1914 in order to "preserve children's faith." This association took upon itself the task of answering all mail marked to Santa Claus, which was handed over to them by the post office. (We got a big kick out of it back at the North Pole. We really did!)

When you get right down to it, it's a lot easier not to believe in Santa Claus. If you don't believe in him, you don't have to define him for yourself. You don't have to decide a lot of other things either. You don't have to worry about how he gets to every single house to deliver his toys in one single night. (Actually it's not such a problem. In Germany, for instance, St. Nicholas comes on December sixth. So not everything has to be done in just one night.)

If you don't believe in Santa Claus, you also don't have to worry about how reindeer fly. But did you know that a hummingbird can hover in place, fly straight up or down, and even backward? One South American species even has a wing beat of up to four thousand, eight hundred strokes a minute! No big deal, you say? It wouldn't be if it wasn't supposed to be impossible for the bird to be able to do it. The trouble is nobody ever bothered to tell the hummingbird that what it was doing was impossible—so it just flies. There may very well be thousands of people who say reindeer can't fly either. The trouble is nobody ever bothered to explain the principles of flight to Dasher, Dancer, and Prancer. So they have absolutely no reason to believe they can't fly. And sometimes what you don't know can be a very big advantage.

The point is, if you don't believe in Santa Claus, you don't have to worry about having one more Christmas thing to worry about! On the other hand, you might consider the fact that you are also missing one of the most special advantages of being young — the joy of freely and unabashedly suspending your disbelief. You may as well! There's precious little encouragement to do it later on. Some biggles have to actually live in a world where the Pennsylvania Dutch aren't Dutch; they're German. Bedstraw isn't straw; it's really an herb that grows wild in the woods and marshes. Catgut strings aren't made from catgut but from sheep intestines. Shooting stars aren't stars; they're meteors and meteorites. And Old Ironsides didn't have iron sides at all. Its sides were made of wood. It's enough to send even a literal person right over the edge! A world like that can make suspending your disbelief feel about the same as doing endless bench presses with very heavy weights.

People's bodies change when they grow—why not their dreams? Their beliefs? To say these things "mature" sounds very nice, but an awful lot of stagnation can hide behind that word *maturity*. To say our dreams and beliefs mature doesn't necessarily mean they have to lose any of their vitality or magic! Do you know what real maturity is anyway? Real maturity is finally getting to that place in life where you're truly ready to begin to learn!

And somebody please explain to me why you humans have come to equate adulthood with the loss of your sense of wonder! What does it mean when someone tells you to act your age? If experience has taught us anything, it is that the more we learn, the more there is to learn. The more we love, the more there is left to love. The more we know, the greater is our sense of wonder at it all! And that wonderment isn't something you should keep to yourself. Shared wonder is one of the greatest joys there is! Life is not a mission you're sent on with sealed orders to be opened only when you've finally made it to your destination. And Santa Claus doesn't die just because we cease to believe in him. The truth is that we are the ones who are diminished by our lack of faith. Dag Hammarskjold once said the same thing about God. Your sense of wonder is always with you. So is God.

And don't you love it when people say you have to put God back into your life—or put God back into the public schools, put God here, put God there. You don't *put* God anywhere! You can't. Besides, God never left. Go and see for yourself if you don't believe me. God's here. God's much closer than you think. Find him again. And dust off your sense of wonder while you're at it. Because if you come close to finding God, you're going to need it.

When you get right down to it, there's not very much wrong with occasionally having visions of sugar plums dancing in your head. And perhaps, from time to time, we all need to believe the moon in the pond is real. All we're really doing is considering the possibilities.

Besides—

> If Santa Claus isn't real,
>> only the literal world is.
>>> Like I said, it's all up to you.

A LESSON FROM THE LILIES

Remember that the most beautiful things in the world are
the most useless; peacocks and lilies for instance.

—JOHN RUSKIN

I f the whole world (south of the North Pole) was suddenly transformed into one single town with one hundred people living in it, fifty of those people would be hungry most of the time. Only fifteen people in that town would be living in adequate housing. Only one of those hundred people would have a college education. Five of the town's senior citizens would be victims of constant physical abuse. Six people, out of the hundred, would control almost half the wealth of that entire town—and of those six, three would be Americans.

On the surface, things might not appear too rosy for this place. Obviously there's some perilous inequality manifesting itself around almost every corner. Fifty people going hungry and eighty-five people without adequate housing can take a serious bite out of Human Dignity. And, if History's shown us anything, it's that people eventually are going to demand to get back a sense of human dignity. It may take a while—because people can endure a great deal of suffering, degradation, and inequality. That's because God made people strong.

But even strength has its limits, and compromise eventually becomes unjustifiable. When that time comes, those fifty hungry people and those eighty-five people living in inadequate housing are going to begin to take a good look around. And the first place they're going to look is in the general direction of those six people who seem to have everything.

The assumption is that if everyone shared equally in everything, there wouldn't be a problem. No one would be greater or lesser than their neighbor. Equal distribution of the wealth would mean there would be food and housing for all. Right? Well, that concept may seem logical on a spreadsheet, but the reality doesn't always balance out quite so nicely. Just ask Lenin.

Let's concentrate, for a moment, on those six people who control most of the wealth of this town. More specifically, let's focus on the three Americans in that group. At least two out of those three Americans are going to tell you they are where they are because of Divine right. If for no other reason, they were born Americans—so they've earned it. America's Declaration of Independence talks about all of you being created equal. This, however, is what's known as a Catch-22. All of you may be created equal; it's just that you don't tend to stay equal—at least not for very long.

The poet Robert Frost once said, "The world is full of willing people, a few willing to work, the rest willing to let them." And you can bet your last nickel that those three Americans have that verse embroidered on a plush, velvet cushion somewhere in their living rooms.

Americans are very clear on one fundamental truth: they have earned whatever it is they have. They earn merit badges and college diplomas. They earn battle wounds and two-week vacations. They earn gold medals and gray hairs. Parents have earned the right to tell their children about how they had to walk five miles to school … in the snow … uphill … both ways. You earn the right to drive a car. (The right to vote in free elections was earned for you. You simply earn the right to keep the privilege.) A middle-aged man suddenly lets his sideburns grow long, buys a sports car, divorces his wife of thirty years, and starts going out with a woman half his age. Why? Because he's earned it. Of course, his wife takes him to court and ends up with half of everything he owns. Why? She's earned it too.

And this word *earned* is always said with a great deal of pride—no matter what the circumstances. And the admonition to go out and earn something for yourself is passed from one person to the next—from one generation to another— like sage advice. "You want something in this world, kid? Get out there and earn it." It's just that—sometimes—that advice gets a slight Marie Antoinette tinge to it.

Now, I'm sure Marie Antoinette didn't say, "Let them eat cake" because she was absolutely heartless. She probably thought she was actually being very kind to the starving peasants. If there was no bread, they'd certainly earned the right to a little cake. Unfortunately, by the time she made that gracious offer, cake was the last thing the peasants wanted to hear about. They'd already gotten a whiff of the filet mignon.

It's just that this earning thing is double edged. By that I mean it doesn't just apply to only the things you want to earn. We also—and to a great degree—earn our wars, slums, poverty, illiteracy, and spiritual starvation. (To name only a few!) You smoke too many cigarettes; you'll probably earn yourself a nice case of lung cancer. It works both ways.

I guess it all boils down to what you do with what you earn that makes the big difference.

Santa Claus and his wife don't have any children of their own. So he simply "adopted" the children of the world. He earned their love and—yes—even their occasional doubts about him as well. (That double-edge again.) It's all part of the territory. The good—the bad. The ying—the yang. The ebb and flow … of everything.

So these six people in this town of one hundred have two choices. Either they sit on their cushions embroidered with Robert Frost's verse on willingness, or they do what they can with what they have to try and make a difference. (If cake is all they have to work with, let's just hope they understand that timing is everything.)

Did you know that Americans give away about one hundred twenty-five billion dollars to charities every year? Well, they do. But before you sit back in the comfortable belief that all Americans are wonderfully generous people, you need to understand a few things about the above figure. The majority of that one hundred twenty-five billion dollars comes from households with incomes well below ten thousand dollars a year! America's poorest households give more than 5 percent of their hard-earned and meager means to charity—even though these gifts obviously involve some degree of sacrifice. On the other hand, the wealthiest Americans, with incomes above one hundred thousand dollars a year, give less than 3 percent.

These figures are troubling when you consider the fact that one of the cornerstones of the holiday season has always been the spirit of giving. Once during each year, everyone is expected to freely open their hearts and share. The truth is, given the prevailing mood, this simple, annual act of unselfishness is becoming harder and harder to realize. Here's what I mean: in 1979, people making one million dollars gave more than 7 percent of their after-tax income to charity. Twelve years later, that figure had dropped to less than 4 percent. Not long ago, eight out of ten Americans who had estates of five hundred thousand dollars or more left absolutely nothing at all to charity. Who knows? Maybe somebody out there finally found a way to take it with them.

And to all of you who annually fret and worry over itemizing deductions on your tax return, take heart! Because heart is obviously something you all have lots of. This is evident in the fact that of all taxpayers who itemize deductions, charitable contributions increased by an average of some 9 percent during the past decade. Again, on the other hand, for those with pretax incomes over one million dollars, contributions decreased by nearly 40 percent.

If peace on earth is something you want, then you truly need to get about the business of earning it. After all, it almost comes one night out of every year without anyone trying very hard at all. Imagine what might happen if people worked on it every day during the rest of the year! And goodwill toward men is going to take some serious concentration too. That's something you earn and keep earning—all your life.

If the world is going to continue to be filled with haves and have-nots, then we've got to be careful about becoming complacent about the prevailing situation. Both sides have got to try to make things better than they are. And the first thing everybody's going to need is a healthy share of human dignity. Because without human dignity, there's no sense of self-worth. And without self-worth, nobody's going to give a flip about changing anything. You know the old saying: apathy is our greatest problem, but who cares!

Do you know who cares in America? Statistics tell us that one hundred million people do! That's right. One hundred million people are out there, waiting to volunteer their time and energy to help make the world a better place. To volunteer, mind you—do it for free. Know what they're waiting for? A leader. Someone to give 'em a unified direction. Someone to say, "Okay, let's do it." Know where you may find that leader? Looked in your mirror lately? I'm serious! Never mind that you don't think you fit the image. Gandhi wasn't exactly what you'd call pin-up material, but he sure made one incredible difference! History books are full of stories about people who changed things—people who, to see them at first glance, didn't exactly appear to be very likely candidates for the job. I mean, for instance, if you were writing down a list of prerequisites for becoming a leader, do you really think one of them would be that you had to have a round little belly that shook when you laughed like a bowl full of jelly? I don't think so. But it's worked extremely well for the boss. (Another example of taking what you have and doing something with it.) And, before you finish stereotyping the role completely, you might also remember that a very wise book reminds us that a child shall lead the way.

In other words, littles have as much of an opportunity to make a difference in this world as biggles. Remember that we're going to try to consider—and remain open to—all of the possibilities. You never know what size or shape your next leader is going to appear to you in. So stay alert; don't preconceive. You don't want to be the one who misses the parade.

And whatever happens, whatever changes we're going to make, need to be made by all of us working together.

Ever heard the word *synergy*? People seem to be using it a lot these days. Basically, *synergy* means that considering the lilies of the field isn't such a bad idea. If you plant two plants next to each other, their roots will naturally commingle. The direct result of this commingling is that the soil improves. The two plants grow better than if they were separated. Thank you, Mother Nature!

The real essence of synergy is that it values differences. It uses differences in an atmosphere of creative cooperation and mutual benefit. Plants are only one part of a larger, natural cycle of life support. If plants thrive, the soil improves. When that happens, other living things benefit. Eventually the entire planet is able to rejuvenate itself—all because two small plants started working together.

Hello! There's a fundamental lesson here!

If it starts somewhere, then somewhere starts with you.

Take a lesson from the lilies! All of us put our roots down sooner or later. We've got to take something from the soil in order to exist. Likewise, we've got to begin to put something back in the process. Otherwise, sooner or later, the soil becomes depleted. And a depleted life support system can't possibly nurture new growth—let alone sustain what's already there.

Americans understood this axiom when they founded their country. How did they put it? "United we stand; divided we fall." The founding father who first came up with that slogan obviously had a few lilies growing in his garden.

Differences can do one of two things. They can keep us separated or bring us together. I'm an elf; you're a human. The differences are obvious. Yet we probably have more things in common than you might realize. Oh, sure, there will always be one or two elves who might say, "I like people well enough. It's just that I wouldn't want my daughter to marry one." And as long as you're a plant who can select what part of the garden you're going to grow in, that sort of thinking will carry you for a certain distance—and no farther.

But a bunch of lilies does not necessarily a garden make. Unless, of course, you're only interested in lily gardens. And lily gardens are quite beautiful. It's just that, usually, gardens contain varieties of things—herbs and plants of different kinds, shapes, sizes, and colors. And each plant, aside from its own intrinsic beauty and uniqueness, has a special contribution to make to the overall life support system of the total environment.

Synergy!

What a wonderful legacy to leave for future generations—an environment that not only allows, but nurtures a true fulfillment of self-worth, a world that has matured into independence by finally embracing the value and necessity of interdependence. Not a bad place to call home. Not a bad place at all!

There used to be a wonderful ceremonial Christmas drink in old England called "lamb's wool." It was a marvelous mixture of hot ale, sugar, spices, eggs, and roasted apples. Sometimes thick cream was also added to this mixture. It was traditionally served in a wassail bowl with pieces of toast floating on top. This is where the terms *toasting someone* or *making a toast* originated. The word *wassail* comes from the Anglo-Saxon *wes hal*, which is another way of saying "be whole." If someone said "wassail" to you, it was customary to reply, "Drink-hail!" That was like saying, "To your health!"

I especially like the literal meaning of "wassail". Be whole! Think about that! If there has ever been a blessing worth sharing or a toast worth making, the literal meaning of this word is certainly one of them! Be whole! What a marvelous challenge to take with us throughout the rest of the year!

Well, it's about time for us to leave our town of one hundred people. As a matter of fact, it's about time for me to leave you. However, as long as this is a town of our own imaginings, we really ought to leave it with something. And I say let's leave 'em with Christmas! Doesn't matter what month of the year it is; we can still leave 'em with a sense of Christmas in their hearts. Whether you are a believer or a nonbeliever, you still have to admit that, for at least one night out of every year, something magical does happen to the world. You can't help but feel it in the air! You can surely see it in the eyes of your children. So we should certainly want to leave our town of one hundred people a bit more in tune with the little inside each of them. We can leave them with hope and, perhaps, a renewed sense of awareness. We can leave them with a certain amount of positive excitement about the future. We should remind them of one of life's greatest truths—that the key to happiness and contentment comes from within. We can leave them with something to put back into the soil of their gardens—something that nurtures the earth!

And who knows? Maybe those three Americans who own most of the wealth in that town will hook up with the other three who own the rest. And maybe—just maybe—those six very wealthy people will find themselves huddled together under some lamp post this year, singing Christmas carols to absolute strangers—or stopping by a soup kitchen to roll up their sleeves and pitch in. We can leave them with the possibility of what can happen once they start using what they have to make the world a better place.

And do you know what? That's a very nice place to leave you, too.

Wassail, my friends!
Be whole!